D09933660

# Empire

On his way out West to find land of his own, Ben Tower finds and rescues beautiful Mattie Sullivan, the lone survivor of a doomed wagon train. Ben and Mattie soon fall in love and plan to travel West to start a new life together.

But the trail westwards is never easy, and wild animals, greedy ranchers, and flash floods are just a handful of the hazards they encounter, not to mention Ben's past catching up with him. Will they ever fulfill their dream of establishing their own little empire in the West?

# Empire

Will Starr

**A Black Horse Western**

ROBERT HALE

© Will Starr 2018
First published in Great Britain 2018

ISBN 978-0-7198-2739-6

The Crowood Press
The Stable Block
Crowood Lane
Ramsbury
Marlborough
Wiltshire SN8 2HR

www.bhwesterns.com

Robert Hale is an imprint
of The Crowood Press

Typeset by
Derek Doyle & Associates, Shaw Heath
Printed and bound in Great Britain by
4edge Limited

*For Carolyn*
*With special thanks to*
*Phyllis and Becky*

# 1

As he topped the small rise, Ben Tower sat his horse a moment and surveyed the mid-western prairie stretched out before him. The late afternoon breezes formed long, rolling waves in the tall grasses, stretching to the horizon in all directions. He hadn't seen a tree in over a week, and the relentless monotony of the grasslands had been known to drive some men insane. Lesser men had taken one look at its empty vastness and gone back home.

To the east, the prairie was vanishing by the day, falling victim to the slow but relentless plow. Trees, once unable to establish roots in the dense grasslands, flourished in the rich soil left by the defeated prairie. But here, the prairie was as untouched and wild as the lone rider who now surveyed it.

Shading his eyes against the sun, he could make out a few small, white splotches several miles to the west. Another slow-moving train of wagons, probably bound for Oregon or California. He would overtake them later today or early in the morning. Maybe he could trade for some coffee and possibly some beans.

Tower was a sometimes cowhand, miner, trapper, and scout for the army. He had grown up in the tough streets of Boston and left town two steps ahead of a street gang and a police detective.

At sixteen years of age, he had fought with a gang member, killed him with his own knife and become a marked man. He had quickly gathered up his few possessions and left in the middle of the night, using the safety of darkness and familiar alleyways to escape.

He headed first south and then west to Pittsburgh where he secured passage as a deck hand on an Ohio River boat, learning the job by doing it. In St. Louis, he joined an expedition overland north to the Missouri, where he found a flatboat captain needing a strong back to help pole upstream. Six weeks later, he joined a party of trappers and headed for the distant mountains, leaving behind all thoughts of Boston and his former life.

His flight to the west proved to be a Godsend. He found that he loved the vast wildness of the land and the ways of western men. He hired out as a buffalo skinner and was taught to shoot by an old mountain man named Jim Bridger. He became a skilled marksman with both rifle and handgun, survived four fights with Plains Indians, and had been wounded twice. He wrestled with wiry Indians and learned their takedowns and holds. He learned how to fight with a knife, cutting edge up and razor-sharp. He had once been trapped by an early mountain snow and spent three months in a cabin stocked with several classic books and an old pile of newspapers. He came out well read, but temporarily ill-tempered. He had crossed Death Valley in the summer and survived a prairie fire in a buffalo wallow. Ben Tower was ready for just about anything.

He was a tall man with broad shoulders and narrow hips. He was aware of women following him with their eyes, but it puzzled him. He wore his hair shoulder-length as was the custom for trappers and buffalo hunters of the time, but, unlike the others, he preferred to be clean-shaven. He was twenty-one years of age and a man full grown.

He sold his pelts and furs in St. Louis for a good price. With part of his stake he bought tools and the gear a man needs for building a home and out buildings. Leading his string of horses and pack-goods, he was once again headed west, but not to trap. This time it was to find some likely-looking rangeland and build a ranch, a life, and a home.

Hours later, Tower topped another rise and immediately spotted a lone wagon less than half a mile away. A few miles farther west he could still see the main group, but they hadn't made much headway and were already halted. In fact, they seemed to be right where he had first spotted them. Maybe they had decided to make early camp. Or maybe there was trouble. They didn't look properly circled for protection, but perhaps they were just resting the stock. Something was not right, so he saw to his weapons. He waited and watched for a long time. Nothing moved and there was no sound. Finally, and warily, he rode down to check on the lone wagon.

He was still a few hundred yards away when he smelled death. He pulled up and slowly looked all around, easing his rifle in its scabbard. Nothing moved and there was no sound but the endless rustling of the grass and the creaking of his saddle leather. Nudging his horse forward, he swung wide of the wagon, eyes moving constantly, looking for danger. He saw and heard nothing but a meadowlark questioning his presence. He walked his mount slowly all the way around the wagon and at last halted, not satisfied but unable to spot trouble. Finally, he climbed to the driver's seat and looked inside. There was a man, a woman, and a small child lying in the wagon bed under blankets. They were all dead at least a day, maybe more.

'You'd best get down from there and stand clear.' The voice was that of a young woman, behind him and to his left. 'I've a rifle and a sore disposition, so keep that in mind. Now you just step down easy and keep your hand away from that pistol.'

Tower climbed slowly down and kept his hands in plain sight. He had no doubt that this woman meant just what she said. And how did he fail to spot her? Where had she hidden herself?

10

'Turn around,' she said, 'and be right careful about it.' There was a great weariness in her voice.

She was seventeen or eighteen and tall for a girl. Her long, black hair was tangled, her face pale with distress, and her dress badly needed washing, yet she was still strikingly beautiful. She was also holding a near-new rifle but the barrel was wavering and weaving. She looked like she was almost out on her feet.

'Name's Ben Tower,' he said quietly. 'I'm bound for the territories and I spotted this wagon, so I came to investigate. What happened here?'

'Do you have any water?'

'I do. Can I fetch it?' He gestured with his head in the direction of his horse, carefully keeping his hands raised and his eyes on her rifle.

She started to speak and then her eyes slowly rolled upward, and she was slumping to the ground when Tower caught her.

He pillowed her head on his blanket roll and wiped her brow with a dampened bandanna. Her eyes opened, and he held a canteen to her lips. 'Just a little at a time. Too much and you might get the cramps.' She nodded and took a few sips. 'If you think you still need your rifle, it's leaning yonder on the wagon wheel.' He smiled.

She eyed him warily but said nothing. She sipped some more water and suddenly made up her mind. She began to talk.

The girl's family had become sick and kept getting

11

sicker. Finally, when it was obvious that they weren't getting any better, the other homesteaders, frightened by suspected cholera, took the team so they couldn't follow and abandoned them. They had also taken the water barrels, reasoning that a dying family had no need for these.

The girl's name was Mattie, and although she showed no sign of illness, they had abandoned her too, just in case. Her mother and little brother had died yesterday morning and her father sometime during the night. Mattie had dug a shallow grave, but was too weak from lack of sleep and water to get them out of the wagon.

Later, while Mattie slept, Tower wrapped them up in their bedding and finished burying them. He said a few words over the graves and when she woke, he got their names, made a marker from the wagon-seat and wired it to a stake. Then he made another sign and posted it on the wagon:

'Cholera. All dead. Keep Away.'

That warning would keep out any human scavengers until he could return.

When Mattie woke again, it was early morning. Ben was slicing bacon into a pan and had coffee made. While they ate, he explained that the rest of the train was only a few miles ahead and wasn't moving. That probably meant they were also sick and unable to proceed.

'I'll ride on ahead and check on them. You'll be fine here until I get back.'

12

'No.' Her answer was firm. 'I'd rather risk getting sick than chance being left behind again.'

Ben looked at her thoughtfully. 'I suppose you're right. If you never got sick the first time, you probably won't now.'

'What about you?'

Ben grinned. 'I don't get sick. I was sick once when I was a boy and I didn't like it much, so I never allowed it again.'

By noon, they were approaching the other wagons and by the odor, realized the worst had happened. Leaving Mattie outside the circle holding his horse, Ben looked in each wagon. Everywhere there was death and he found no one alive. In the distance, he spotted a small herd of horses which would be the wagon teams and a few riding horses. He also saw two or three milk cows on a slope to the north. In the west, clouds were beginning to build, and the storm looked like a soaker. That was good news. He needed the rain for what he had to do.

'I'm going to gather up a team to pull all the wagons tight together,' he told Mattie. 'After it rains, I'm going to put the bodies in the wagons and burn them.' Mattie looked at him, shocked. 'I can't bury all those folks,' he explained, 'we'd run out of food and water long before I finished. Besides, the wagons will carry the sickness too and also need to be burned. This storm will soak the grass so it won't catch and start a prairie fire. For now, let's set up a camp before the rains come.

'I'll take you back east to your kinfolk. This is no place for a woman alone.' The rain drummed steadily on the tarp stretched over their small fire and in the distance, lightning flashed silently.

'I have no kin', she said simply, 'and no home to go to. Pa sold everything we had for this trip.' She glanced at Ben. 'I'll go with you if you'll allow it. I have no other choice.' Ben nodded and added another buffalo chip to the fire.

'I'm not sure where I'm going, Mattie, but I have big plans.'

'One thing,' said Mattie. She lifted her chin and looked directly at Ben. 'I am a lady.'

Ben grinned. 'Well, I may look rough, Mattie, but beneath the bark, I'm all gentleman.'

The next morning, with the grass still wet, they poured lamp oil and kerosene on the wagons and set them ablaze. Then they returned to Mattie's wagon and burned it too. Later, they passed the still-smoldering remnants of the main party of wagons, gathered up the remaining stock, and headed west toward the pale, blue mountains just now showing their faraway peaks on the distant horizon.

For weeks, they rode west by southwest, fording small streams and swimming larger ones. Several times they spotted buffalo, and twice, Indians, but they kept their distance. 'They probably think we're a large party with all this stock,' Ben said. 'If they knew it was just one man and a woman, they'd probably try to raid us, but then again, maybe not.

14

They're notional.'

The prairie seemed endless, and Mattie found the monotony of the tall grasses disturbing, but Ben seemed at home with it. He was ever vigilant, pausing now and then to watch their back trail. In the late afternoons, he habitually picked out a camp-site that they could defend if necessary, and where they could see without being seen.

Late one afternoon, while Ben was digging a rock out of a hoof, Mattie spoke softly to him from the small hill where she was keeping watch.

'I see some deer to the south. Should I take one?'

'How far off?'

'About two hundred yards.'

'That's a long shot. Think you can hit one that far off?'

Mattie glanced at him briefly, and then brought her rifle to her shoulder and fired, all in one easy motion.

'He's down. We'll have fresh meat tonight.'

Ben walked up the slope and followed her point-ing finger. The downed deer was at the base of another small hill, and was every bit of two hundred yards away. He found himself staring at Mattie with a new-found respect. She looked up at him, and for the first time since they'd met, she had a small smile on her face.

'Where did you aim?'

'It was a heart shot. I hit where I'm aiming.'

She was right. The buck had been killed instantly

15

by a bullet through the heart. That night, they had deer liver with some wild onions Ben had found. He butchered the rest of the carcass, and smoked it over his fire. It would help it keep for a few days, and what they did not need he placed on a flat rock.

'Somebody might come along hungry.'

At her questioning glance, Ben explained.

'We're probably being watched. There are several Plains tribes around here. This is to let them know I'm aware of them. That way, they won't think we're easy prey and will be cautious about attacking us.'

The land sloped gently but ever upward and after two weeks, they were in the foothills of the great western mountains. The long grasses gradually gave way to scrubby brush and then trees. They were in a magnificent new land and breathtaking beauty was everywhere. They passed streams roaring with white-water storm runoff and giant bluffs of sheer granite. Daily, they spotted deer and elk and once they saw a large black bear foraging for berries, and gave him a wide berth.

One cool morning while Mattie cleaned up after a breakfast of bacon, biscuits, and coffee, Ben took his glass and climbed to the brow of the hill to scout the trail. After a few minutes he motioned Mattie to join him. As she approached, he held a finger to his lips for silence. Peering over the crest, Mattie spotted the smoke of a small fire.

Ben studied the small party camped under a giant cottonwood. That they were Indians, he had no doubt, however, they looked anything but hostile. There was an old man and woman and someone lying on a travois. Their lone horse grazed quietly nearby, and he looked as old as his owners. Ben glassed the surrounding hills for half an hour more but saw no sign. At last he returned to Mattie and mounted.

'They're Indians that's certain, but my guess is that they're in bad shape. We'll ride on down and see.'

The Indians heard Ben and Mattie approaching but gave no sign. Ben dismounted and spoke rapidly in Cheyenne. After five minutes of conversation, he returned to Mattie.

'The man on the travois is their son, a warrior. He was wounded in a skirmish with an army patrol and they couldn't keep up with the rest of the camp. They're very tired and have no food.'

Ben walked back to his packhorses and removed a haunch of venison from a deer he had shot earlier. He walked up to the old woman and dropped it at her feet. He then bent over the young warrior and lifted his shirt. After a moment, he said something to the warrior and the young man nodded his head weakly, staring at Mattie. He had never seen a white woman and even in his pain, was fascinated.

'The bullet went clear through the fleshy part of his waist. I don't think it hit anything vital, but it is infected,' Ben told Mattie. 'I've some powders that an army doctor gave me. I'll try some on the wound.

It may not work but it can't make it any worse.'

After pouring the powder into the bullet hole, Ben bound the wound with some cloth bandages the doctor had given him. Then he roped two of the horses they had brought from the doomed wagon train and led them back to the warrior's camp. He nodded at the Indians and he and Mattie rode off. When they made camp that night, Mattie spoke of the Indians over supper.

'What did they say to you? Did they thank you?'

'They don't think like white men. They're probably wondering why we didn't just kill them and take their horse. They certainly would have. They answered my questions, but they had none for me.'

'But you helped them anyway?'

Ben shrugged. 'Even Indians need help now and then, but their ways are not my ways. I just made it look like I didn't care one way or the other so as not to shame them. That's why we rode off and didn't look back. The way of the Indian is an old way, and a hard way, Mattie, but it's also a good way. However, it's a way that is doomed. They've roamed this land for thousands of years, foraging and taking buffalo and game where they find it and when they find it. Sometimes they feast and sometimes they starve, but they survive by always moving on.

'To them, the land belongs to everyone and yet to no one. Their real enemy is not the soldier, but the plow and the fence. Farmers, miners, and ranchers are coming, and they will keep on coming until all the land is claimed and all the buffalo killed to make way for the white man's cattle, his crops, and his fences. It's not right and it's also not wrong. It just is.

'The Indians have no concept of the number of white men who will be coming. They don't understand the ways of the white man and the white man does not understand them. The centuries of freely wandering the plains are almost over. It's sad, but it's also inevitable.'

Mattie nodded and stirred the stew. After a long silence, she spoke without lifting her head.

'I never thanked you proper for helping me, Ben. If you hadn't come along, I'd likely have starved or died of thirst by now.'

'I didn't have much choice with a big rifle pointed at me.' Ben smiled. 'Besides, a man doesn't often find a beautiful girl to rescue in the middle of the plains.'

'I've been told that I'm pretty.' Mattie blushed, looking at her hands. She raised her eyes to Ben. 'But it never meant much to hear it until now.'

Ben lit his pipe and looked off into the distance. 'I've been alone most all of my life, Mattie. My father and mother died when I was about eleven and I had no other kin. I found a job cleaning a stable in Boston and slept in the loft. The owner taught me to read and loaned me books. That was my education.

'I had a run-in with a gang member when I caught him trying to steal a horse out of the stable. He pulled a knife on me, but I knocked it out of his hand with a pitchfork. He grabbed an axe and I killed him with his own knife. The stable owner gave me some money and told me to leave Boston immediately because the man I killed had kin who would surely be hunting me. I headed west.'

Ben waved his pipe at the land and looked over at Mattie.

'I've ridden the trails for weeks without seeing another soul and it never bothered me much. A man can be complete within himself and needing no one for a time. But then, life is about building something that will last, and it needs to be shared to make it complete. For that, a man needs to care for someone other than himself. Someone who will be his equal and his companion. Someone he can respect and admire.'

He smiled at her. 'I've never looked for such a woman, Mattie. I figured that one day she'd just show up.'

The sun was already setting beyond the great peaks now towering close to them. The heat of the day quickly gave way to the chill of the high country. Their small fire was down to coals and somewhere to the south a pack of coyotes yipped frantically over a kill. Ben poured a cup of coffee for Mattie and himself.

'I'll miss the green of Ohio,' said Mattie, pulling her shawl tighter against the cool air, 'but I love this land even more. The vastness of it all is a little frightening but it's also exciting. I never knew I had adventure in me until now. I suppose I got that from my father.'

She cupped her hands around the coffee and the warmth felt good.

'Pa was a restless man. We had a good, bottom-land farm in Ohio with a solid barn and house, and we wanted for nothing, except for Pa. He longed for the great unknown, and he spoke often of the western mountains of an evening. He talked excitedly of the faraway places he had heard about from the adventurers who stopped by from time to time. Ma was happy with what we had, but she knew her man, so she quietly made plans for the move she knew would surely come someday.'

Ben nodded and fed a few small sticks to the fire.

Mattie sipped her coffee. 'Then one day last winter, Pa got word of a group organizing an expedition and Ma told me that we would be leaving in the spring. We had a sale, and Pa bought our wagon and team with some of the proceeds and banked most of the rest.' She looked straight into Ben's eyes. 'He carried over a thousand dollars in gold in a money belt. I took it when they died and I'm wearing it.'

He looked up from the fire. 'Yes, I know. When you fainted and I caught you, I felt it around your waist, and I figured it for what it was. It's your money, Mattie. I have no claim on it nor do I want one. I have other plans.' In the glow of the fire, Ben thought he saw a fleeting smile cross her lips, before she continued.

'The trip went well at first, with folks being right friendly, but after we crossed the big river and started across that prairie, people began keeping to themselves. The mood got sullen, and there were several fights among the men. Instead of one or two main fires, folks began building their own fire next to their wagon, and the sharing of food in a pot luck fashion halted. Only the children still played together, and even that often brought a sharp word from parents for no good reason.

'Then Ma took sick with the fever. The next day, it was Timmy, my little brother. Word got around quickly and folks started glancing at our wagon and muttering under their breath. Pa took to keeping his pistol close to hand and bade me do the same with my rifle. Then Pa woke up with the fever too, and the wagon folks had themselves a meeting. They robbed us and then deserted us for dead. I thought about taking a few of them with my rifle, but it would have done no good.

'My brother died first, then Ma, and late that night, Pa died along with his dreams of the new lands and that left me alone for the first time in my life. I was some scared, and didn't sleep that night, but I had to bury my family and decide what to do about staying alive. I dug what grave I could manage, but I was too exhausted to bury them. I hadn't slept since Ma got sick, and I couldn't bed down in the wagon, so I made up a bed in the grass and was just about to nod off when you rode up.'

Ben smiled. 'I guess that explains why I didn't see you and let you get the drop on me like that.'

Ben handed Mattie a stick with a chunk of fire-roasted venison speared on it.

'Someday all this land will be tamed and civilized, Mattie. But before that happens and while I'm among the first to see it, I'm going to stake out my own patch and build as big as I can. All this is here for the taking for the man that can hold it, and that's what I intend to do.'

'Where will you settle, Ben?'

'I'll know it when I see it.' He paused, moving the coffeepot to a cooler spot. 'I'm telling you all this for a reason, Mattie.' He gazed at her through the light smoke of their fire. 'I want you to be there with me. I've fallen in love with you, Mattie.'

Mattie looked off at the peaks, glowing red in the last moments of the sunset. 'I never told you this, Ben, but I woke up as you finished the burying of my family and I watched as you knelt and prayed over the graves of complete strangers. It was the act of a good and kindly man and I fell in love with you at that moment. My answer is yes, Ben. Wherever you go, I'll be with you and we'll build it together.'

She looked at him and smiled. 'But first we marry!'

'Of course, sweetheart.' He grinned. 'I wouldn't have it any other way. And you won't even need your rifle!'

Later that night, as Ben brought an armload of

dead wood to the fire, he saw Mattie standing near the edge of the firelight, silently looking off to the east. He put down his fuel and walked up to her, softly placing his arm around her shoulders. After a brief hesitation, she leaned against him.

'I wish Pa could have seen all this, Ben. It was his dream.' She was silent for a moment and then she looked up at Ben. 'You and Pa would have liked each other. You are very much like him, and that's a compliment.'

For a long time, they stood quietly, her cheeks damp with tears. Ben realized that it was the first time since he'd met her that she had allowed herself to grieve. Ben bent down and gently kissed her forehead. As he started to move away, Mattie whirled around and threw her arms around his neck, kissing him fiercely on the lips. Then she stepped back and looked him in the eyes. 'I'm no prude, Ben. I have the same longings that you do, and I will happily give myself to you as your wife. But I'll give myself to no man unless he's willing to marry me first.'

Ben smiled at her. 'I would have been disappointed had you said anything else.'

Mattie saw the valley first. A slide across the narrow mountain trail had caused them to backtrack so they took a route with no trail, chancing they'd locate another way. They'd traveled some ten miles and were about to top a ridge when Ben noticed a pack that needed re-lashing. While he worked on it,

Mattie rode on ahead, dismounted and carefully crept up to peer over the ridge as Ben had taught her. For a long time, she just sat and stared. Then she called to him.

On the far side of the ridge was a spectacular, sweeping valley, stretching out to the south for at least twenty miles and perhaps fifteen miles wide. It was bordered on both the east and west by heavily-wooded slopes of tall, straight pines and here and there, stands of aspen. A small river flowed from a hidden source somewhere to the north and its banks were lined with giant cottonwoods. The valley floor itself was green and lush. With his glass, Ben could make out a small herd of wild horses. He saw no one and no sign of civilization. He sat back and took a deep breath.

'Here it is, Mattie. We'll build here.'

# 2

For the next two weeks, they worked from dawn to dusk, putting up a small cabin near the western slope where they could enjoy the morning sun. It was also an easily-defended location and not too far for the horses to snake the building logs. There was also a nearby spring that could be reached if need be, even under fire.

Ben laid a foundation of flat rocks and built walls of logs carefully selected, cut off the slopes, and snaked back down to the site with a team. Using his own tools and some salvaged from the doomed wagon train, he skinned the logs and squared them up. He sawed planks for windows, doors, shelves and rough furniture.

The door and windows were constructed to be quickly bolted and shuttered should they be attacked. Gun ports covered all four walls, and were also easily shuttered. It was a wild country, and a man had to make preparations. Their few possessions and

26

the horses would be a bonanza to a war party, and there were always the roving thieves and murderers. Both Mattie and Ben kept their rifles close to hand at all times.

They worked together to raise the roof poles and then Ben sawed eighteen-inch sections from two large logs and began the monotonous job of splitting shingles for their roof.

Mattie took it upon herself to level the dirt floor and then tile it with flagstones she found. She grouted it with a mixture of dirt, clay, dried grass, manure, and water. In amazement, Ben watched her from his crude, shingle-splitting bench.

'I saw Pa do this. We had dirt floors and Ma hated them, so Pa put in some stone. I'd live on dirt floors if I had to, but why do that when a little work can make up a fine floor?'

Mattie looked at the growing pile of shingles and glanced at the roof. 'How many will it take, Ben? That looks like a great plenty to me.'

'I doubt that's even half enough, Mattie. They overlap quite a bit, but I'll start shingling tomorrow, and we'll see.'

It was just over half enough, but one side was done, which pleased her immensely. He split another large pile and then showed Mattie how to split while he began roofing the remaining side. In the end, they had enough shingles left over to cover the small porch roof.

For the fireplace and hearth, Ben selected rocks

that wouldn't explode when heated. He made two beds but separated them with a curtain. Mattie was adamant about a wedding and Ben respected her for it. He cut leather hinges for windows and doors and then one day, the cabin was complete.

The next day, Ben found Mattie still in bed when he returned from feeding the stock. One touch of her forehead told him she was seriously ill. For a solid week she was delirious, racked with a high fever and a deep, rasping cough. Ben alternately cooled her with damp rags and wrapped her in blankets when she shivered with chills. While she slept fitfully, he gathered various herbs and roots as Indians had shown him, and made teas and broths for her to drink. It seemed to help the fever, although she was still weak and exhausted.

Then one morning he rose to find Mattie sitting on the porch bench, sipping a cup of coffee. He thought the worst was over. But the next morning, he was unable to rise.

'I'm sorry, Mattie. I said I never take sick, but I reckon I let my guard down.'

Mattie was still weak, but she tended to Ben as well as she could. She knew they were in serious trouble. They were out of meat because he hadn't hunted while she was sick, and she had no idea what plants he had gathered to treat her. His fever raged and all she could do was try to keep him cool and give him sips of water. She opened the corral gate and let the horses out to fend for themselves, knowing that she had neither the time nor the energy to feed them. Ben wouldn't like it, but it couldn't be helped.

After a week, a delirious Ben was still very ill and seemed to be failing when Mattie heard riders outside the cabin. Catching up her rifle, she stepped out the door in time to confront four warriors.

For a long moment, they just stared at each other. They had not expected a woman and certainly not a white woman with a rifle. Then an older-looking brave spoke up.

'Where your man?'

'He's inside,' said Mattie, 'he's sick.'

He turned and gazed at the horses grazing far to the south and then nodded at her rifle.

'You give us long gun. We take horses. Then we go.'

'I will not.'

'Then we take and burn cabin!'

'You make war on women and sick men? Are you warriors or coyotes?'

A younger brave suddenly kneed his horse forward and peered at Mattie intently for a moment. He spoke to the older one. The older one snorted angrily but turned away. They rode off.

Puzzled, Mattie watched them go and then almost collapsed from fatigue and fear. She stepped back inside and began again to mop Ben's fevered brow with a damp rag. Hours later, she again heard the beat of unshod hoofs. Picking up her rifle, and this time angry through and through, she stepped outside. If they still wanted trouble, they could damn well have it!

The young warrior was back but alone this time. He reached behind him and threw a haunch of fresh venison at her feet. Then he held out a handful of herbs and plants and grunted at her. He made signs to make a tea out of them and give it to Ben. She took them and stepped back, bewildered. The young brave fixed her with his coal-black eyes and lifted his buckskin shirt to reveal an ugly but fully-healed bullet wound. Ben's doctoring had apparently worked. After seeing the scar, she recognized the warrior as the young, wounded man on the travois. When Mattie nodded her understanding, the warrior wheeled his mount and rode off without looking back.

She made the herbal tea and some broth from a piece of the venison and spooned it slowly to Ben. The next day, his improvement was obvious. Within a week, he was back on his feet, weak, but much better. Mattie was also weak, but they were alive. That was enough.

For the next two months, Ben built corrals and cut hay. They were in snow country, and he wanted adequate feed for the winter. He heaped up two large stacks, ever watchful for danger, but he saw no one. He and Mattie were alone in the vastness of Tower Valley.

He scouted the east slopes and found a natural pond. It was fairly large and perfect for watering stock with its rocky, but gently sloping banks and tall cottonwoods. The small river was fed from several small streams to the north and looked to be year-round and dependable. He followed it downstream, and found several places where it was safe to ford, but even those places had at least two feet of water. With its abundant grasses and plentiful water, the valley was ideal for a cattle ranch, and a big one at that.

He was marking trees for timber cutting when a flash caught his eye. Mattie was using a mirror far below to get his attention. Ben waved, and Mattie pointed down the valley to the south. Looking that way, Ben spotted a lone rider with a pack horse and was instantly ashamed that he had missed the man's approach himself. Something like that could get them killed. He silently vowed to be more watchful.

He mounted his horse and began making his way back to the cabin. Mattie met him at the door with her rifle and they watched as the stranger rode up, looking all around and noting the well-built cabin and haystack, with obvious approval.

'Howdy folks. Name's Jim Stillwell but most folks just call me Bear on account of a fight I had with one a few years back. I won.'

He was a tall, thin man with slightly stooped shoulders, long, gray hair, and a tobacco-stained beard. His buckskins were marked with the sweat and grime of many miles on many trails. He looked to be about fifty, although his eyes were sharp and quick with

31

mischievous humor.

'Light and set,' Ben replied. 'I'm Ben Tower and this is Mattie Sullivan.' At the puzzled look on Bear's face, Mattie said, 'We are to be married as soon as we find a preacher.'

'Ben Tower, eh? Heard of you. You rode with Bridger some?'

Ben nodded, surprised. He had no idea that he'd gained a reputation. 'That's right. We hunted buffalo.'

'Needin' a preacher, eh? Well then, you're in luck! There's a new town by the name of Cook's Crossin' just sprung up awhile back, 'bout twenty-five miles southwest of here and they have 'em a sky pilot, church and all!'

'Do they have a store?' Ben asked. 'We're needing to put in supplies for winter.'

'Store? Why they have two stores, three saloons, and a sawmill. Some of 'em come in on a wagon train two years ago and while they was waitin' for the spring melt to slow down so's they could ford the river, they just up and decided that they had come far enough and they built the town right there! Since then, two more wagon trains joined 'em and now they have a right nice town. They even have a bank!'

'I'll be wanting to buy cattle come spring,' Ben replied. 'Breeding stock and young stuff. I'm going to make a ranch out of this valley,' he said, sweeping his arm.

'It's a fair lookin' land sure enough,' said Bear thoughtfully, looking all around. 'I wonder why nobody never claimed it afore this?' He spat on the ground and rubbed his beard.

'Mostly trappers and mountain men is all that's ever seen it, I reckon,' he said finally. 'Probably just never occurred to 'em to stake it out.'

Bear took a cup of coffee and sat on the porch rail. Looking off to the west he was deep in thought and then seemed to make up his mind about something. 'You say you're needin' cattle huh? There's a hangin' valley some fifty odd miles west of here with some two hunnert 'n fifty head for the takin'. Least wise they were there 'bout ten year ago.'

'How did they get there?' asked Ben.

'Well,' said Bear, with a twinkle in his eye, 'me and my brother found us a bunch of un-branded strays and we sort of drifted 'em off in that direction before anybody else could put an iron to 'em or hang us. I knowed me a trail up the side of a mesa to that hangin' valley I spoke of and we sort of pushed them cows on up there. They been there ever since, far as I know. The grass and water was good so there'd be no reason to leave unless someone pushed 'em out.'

'What's your price? And what about your brother's share?'

'Well, Tommy got hisself foolishly killed down in Sonora, nigh on eight years ago. Now me, I'm gettin' on in years and I been sorta lookin' for a likely place

33

to spend the rest of my days.' He pointed off to a small, grassy knoll about a mile to the north. 'I'll ride with you to fetch 'em cows if you'll allow me to build me a cabin over yonder. After that, I'll pay my keep by workin' around your ranch. You'll find that I'm right handy.'

He raised his eyes to them. 'I'm weary of livin' alone. I'll trade you 'em cows for another cup of coffee and a place to live out my days.'

'Ben,' said Mattie later that night, 'let's go to the Crossing and stock up on supplies and then you and Bear go gather those cattle while I tend the cabin and stock.'

'First things first,' said Ben as he smiled, 'let's go to the Crossing and look up that preacher. We'll be needing some strong sons if we hope to make a go of this ranch.'

Mattie blushed, and then retorted with a smile. 'And I'll be needing a daughter or two to help feed all you men!'

Ben looked down at her and took her small hands in his. 'We'll have us a good family and a good life, Mattie. It's written in the book.'

The people of Cook's Crossing had spent most of their time building a town and settling in, so the wedding of Ben and Mattie provided the needed excuse for a well-earned shindig.

Ben pulled his black, broadcloth suit out of his pack, and had it brushed and cleaned by the woman who ran the laundry. One of the women discovered that Mattie had no wedding dress, and took her home.

'I made this before we came west, dear.' She gazed away for a moment and tears welled in her eyes. 'It was to have been my daughter Annie's wedding dress, but she died on the trail.' She looked back at Mattie and smiled wistfully. 'She would have wanted someone like you to have it. She was a lovely girl, with a loving heart. You remind me of her.'

The woman's name was Mrs O'Hara, and Mattie cried with her over her loss. The dress fit perfectly, and when Mrs O'Hara saw Mattie in the gown, tears filled her eyes and they cried again.

The small church was packed. Weddings and funerals were major events, so everybody came from miles around. Women wore their Sunday best, while most of the men wore their best work clothes, with hair slicked back above their ruddy, sunburned faces. Small boys chased one another while small girls turned up their noses and pretended to ignore them.

Ben had faced harsh winters, street gangs, and raging rivers, but wearing a suit and standing up in front of all those people scared him some. Bear, his best man, was openly terrified. But when the pianist began playing the Bridal Chorus, Ben turned to see Mattie coming down the aisle in her wedding dress, and all else faded into the background. She was stunningly beautiful, and a quiet gasp murmured through the crowd.

She was escorted by Mr O'Hara, since she was wearing the dress meant for his daughter, and because her own father would have approved of him. When the preacher asked who was giving Mattie's hand to Ben in marriage, George O'Hara smiled down at her gently and quietly murmured, 'I do.'

Josephine O'Hara, Annie's thirteen-year-old younger sister, was delighted at Mattie's invitation to be Maid of Honor, and proudly stood beside her as Preacher Hanson began to recite the age-old rite of uniting man and wife in holy matrimony. The older ladies cried, and the younger ones looked on in envy. The marriage-aged, single males were wide-eyed, and silently promising themselves to stay far away from eligible young ladies, at least for as long as they could hold out.

When the ceremony ended, the preacher smiled and said, 'You may kiss the bride.'

Ben bent and brushed her lips lightly, but Mattie would have none of it. She put her arms around his neck and kissed him soundly, and the crowd laughed. 'I've waited a long time to kiss my man and you'll not short me now that the time has come,' she whispered. At Ben's startled look, she laughed for the first time since he had met her, and it was a beautiful laugh. Ben suddenly realized he had met his match and more. Mattie Tower was proving to be quite a woman.

There were three fiddle players and two square-dance callers and Mattie turned out to be a dancer. One by one, the men showed up for their dance with the bride, so it was late in the evening before they were able to steal away to the room provided to them by Preacher Hanson and his wife.

Ben shut the door and put his arms around Mattie, kissing her with meaning, releasing the pent-up emotions that had been building ever since that long-ago day he'd found her on the prairie, alone and frightened. It was early in the morning before sleep finally won over.

While Mattie shopped for supplies the next day, Ben had a drink at the Trail's End saloon where he listened to idle gossip about wagon trains, cattle prices in Kansas, and talk of a nearby railroad coming through. He wondered why the railroad would pass near the town when a much better route was available some fifty miles to the north.

After his drink, he wandered around town, stopping to talk to the various merchants and the sawmill operator. For a while, he watched the construction of a ferry, large and strong enough to transport two wagons at a time across the river, maybe even in flood stage. Cook's Crossing was thriving.

He was nearing the Trail's End when he heard a shout and a smash from inside the saloon. A red-headed hard-case he had noted earlier in the day, crashed through the bat-wing doors with a gun in his hand and his back to Ben. On a hunch, Ben tripped him, and he went sprawling into the dusty street, gun flying. Instantly Ben had him in a hammerlock and marched him back into the saloon.

'He pulled a gun and stole the cash from the till,' shouted the excited saloonkeeper. 'Then he pistol-whipped a man who tried to stop him.'

'Who's the law around here?' asked Ben.

'There ain't no law and there ain't no jail. We ain't got around to it yet.'

'Well, I can't hang on to him forever. What do you want to do with him?'

'We built us an ice house for next year,' said the saloonkeeper, 'but it's still empty so I guess we can keep him in there until the U.S. marshal shows up next month.'

'That ain't no way to treat a man,' protested the hard-case. 'There ain't even a window for a man to look out!'

'I reckon you should have considered that before you robbed the saloon,' said Ben, 'let's go.'

The redhead bared yellow teeth and glared at Ben 'I'll kill you for this. Nobody puts a hand on me and lives.'

'Well, I'm still breathing.'

Later, as Ben and Mattie prepared to return to the ranch, the saloonkeeper drove up in a buckboard.

'My name's Jacob Talley and this here is sort of a wedding present,' he said gruffly, 'and it's my way of thanking you for getting my money back. I don't have no use for this here buckboard anymore and it just ain't fitting for your wife to have to ride astride wherever she goes. So, take it on home with you and just return my team next time you're in town.'

He spun on his heel abruptly, and strode rapidly away from an astonished Ben and Mattie.

'I can't let him do that, Mattie. I have to return this.'

'You'll do no such thing. He felt like this was the right thing to do and you'll not take that pleasure away from him. Now let's go home.'

Ben stared at his new wife with a dawning understanding of who she was. Then he shrugged his shoulders. 'All right, Mrs Tower. Let's go home.'

Ben and Mattie sat on the porch with Bear, taking their morning coffee and watching the rising sun.

'I made a deal with Ollie Sampson, the sawmill owner,' said Ben. 'I'm to deliver logs to his mill in exchange for sawn boards and timber, and later on, cash money.'

'But that's fifteen miles or so, Ben,' replied Mattie. 'What will we use to deliver timber?'

'We won't. We'll just mark and float the logs down our river to where it joins the larger river to Cook's Crossing and then downstream to the mill. I made a deal with the ferry operator to snag what the mill misses and hold them for Sampson. I've already selected enough timber to satisfy the contract for the next two years. We'll cut them, snake them to the stream, and let them float clear to the mill. I've scouted the stream, and other than a couple of spots where we'll have to clean out some roots and old flood jams, we should only have an occasional snag to deal with.'

Bear turned out to be a good hand with both a double-bitted axe and a two-man saw. Together, he and Ben made good the contract for an entire year's supply of saw logs for the mill in less than three months. Twice they had to clear jams at a particularly sharp curve in the river, and once where it widened and became fairly shallow. After two months, Bear rode into Cook's Crossing to check on the delivery and found a mounting pile of logs and a happy mill owner. The ferry operator had built a second ferry with his cut of the timber and brought in a steam-powered donkey engine to operate the cables. While Bear watched, a log floated in and the operator retrieved it. He checked the markings and discovered that it had taken just over four days to float to the mill.

With the log contract satisfied, Ben made ready to begin stocking the ranch. 'We'd best go and gather those stray cattle Bear spoke of, before winter,' he told Mattie. 'Do you want to go to the Crossing and stay with the O'Hara family until we get back?'

'No, I'll stay here. If I need anything, I have a team and the buckboard. When will we get our lumber for the house and barns?'

'It'll be next spring. Those logs are green and will need to season out before they're milled. Ollie

Sampson will deliver them come May and we'll start raising the house and barns soon after.'

'That'll work out just about right.'

'Why do you say that?'

'Because by then you'll be a father.'

He stared at her, slack-jawed. 'Are you sure?'

Mattie shook her head in disgust. 'Of course I'm sure! A woman knows these things.'

'Boy or girl?'

'Yes. Now go wash up for supper.'

## 3

Mattie's revelation that she was with child changed everything, so over her protests, Ben arranged for the O'Hara family to check on her periodically. Then Josephine spoke up and volunteered to stay with Mattie until Ben returned, an offer that Mattie quickly accepted. She was, after all, just a few years older than Josephine and they had quickly become close friends.

Mattie had carefully packed away her wedding dress after the ceremony and later, given it back to the O'Hara family. When Mrs O'Hara protested, Mattie silenced her with a hug.

'This dress was meant for Annie O'Hara, and then loaned to me out of great kindness, and I wore it with pride. Now I return it to the O'Hara family so that it can be worn by Josephine when some lucky boy wins her heart. It's the way it was meant to be.'

The air was cold and brisk under a cloudless sky on

the morning of departure. Ben and Bear made final preparations and saddled up. Each man had a string of three horses, two pack horses and a second riding horse. Bear carried a Sharps .50 buffalo rifle, and two side arms, one under his belt and another in his pocket. He also carried a short-barreled shotgun in his bedroll. Ben carried his Winchester in a saddle boot and two revolvers, one on his side and one hidden in his waistband.

Ben had put out a call for extra hands to help on the drive, but it was branding season and all available men were working. He had also approached an older man who had worked the trails as a cook, and still owned a chuck wagon.

'You're welcome to borrow my wagon, gents, but these old bones have been jostled enough following the dust on cattle drives. It's a young man's game.'

His eyes twinkled.

'I found me a widder-woman what owns a small restaurant and was looking for a good cook. Reckon I'll just stay here and see how that shapes out. But like I said, you kin borrow the wagon.'

Ben nodded to Bear, and walked with Mattie to the site where he planned to build the big house and barns. It was on a flat bench that sloped slightly away to the south and was high enough to see the entire valley. Recent rains had spurred growth, and the area was resplendent with wild flowers.

'Keep your eyes open and pay attention to the horses, Mattie. They'll usually spot things first and let you know. That pup is also getting to the point where he'll start to let you know when someone's around, so pay attention to him too.'

'You've told me all this many times, Ben. I'll not forget. You and Bear just go get our cattle, and don't worry about me. Remember that deer I shot? That was no accident. I can do it time and again.'

'I know, Mattie, but a man worries about such things. Let's walk back and we'll be on our way.'

'Ben?'

He turned to look at her, and saw that it was true what they said about a woman with child; they have a glow about them. He waited.

'Are you going to leave without telling me you love me? A woman wants to hear it, now and then.'

Ben put his arms around her and held her close.

'I grew up with no one, Mattie, no family at all, so I'm not used to such things. Forgive me if I sometimes neglect to tell you how much I love you.'

The ride to Bear's hanging valley took them across high desert and an occasional stream with at least a little grass. Ben saw that the drive would have to allow time for the herd to feed and water when and where it was available. Bear pointed out landmarks and they paused now and then to study their back trail. They weren't expecting trouble, but cautious men tend to live longer. Once they spotted several Indians who appeared to be moving camp and not looking for trouble.

Several times they saw deer, and once, a small pack of wolves that appeared to be on the hunt. Antelope dotted the grassy plain areas and eagles hunted overhead. It was a beautiful and immense land. Bear pointed out a far range of mountains, blue with distance.

'That there hangin' valley is on a mesa just behind 'em ridges, yonder. It'll take us south of Crested Butte and north of the Powderhorn. It's some fair rugged country, but there'll be water and good grass, time to time.'

On the first night, they camped on a protected ledge and Ben spotted lights far off to the south. 'That there's an old ranch belongs to a Mexican feller name of Rodriguez. Me and my brother ate there one time when we was ridin' the grub line.' Bear grinned. 'If'n you ever have a hankerin' for beef, beans and tortillas that'll melt in your mouth, we'll ride on down that way sometime.'

They were up and in the saddle by daybreak, following a trail Bear knew, when they spotted a party of warriors making their way down a dry wash. They detoured north and picked up another trail, following it for some ten miles before swinging back to Bear's trail. They rode alert for several miles, but the war party never appeared. Bear cut a chew off a plug and leaned forward in the saddle to ease his tired legs.

'They was young bucks, lookin' to win 'emselves a name and impress the young squaws. They ain't as wily as the older men, but they can kill you just as dead.' He spat over his shoulder. 'This here route will take us to that mesa without crossin' too many ridges and sky-linin' ourselves, unless you got another idea.'

'I'm following you, Bear. Lead the way.'

They travelled the trail onto a high, desert plain, with sparse grasses and occasional prickly pear. They were nearly five-thousand feet up, and there was a cool bite to the dry air. A pale sun offered little heat, and when they camped that night under a twisted cedar, it was cold.

Bear pulled a harmonica out of his pack, played several old, Irish songs, and was surprised when Ben began to sing the words in a fair, tenor voice. At his look, Ben smiled. 'I grew up in Boston with the Irish, so I know their music and dances. But don't tell Mattie, or she'll expect me to dance an Irish jig or two.'

Bear looked at him through his bushy brows. 'Well, can you dance them jigs?' he asked.

'Of course I can. But don't you dare tell Mattie.' He scowled a warning at Bear, who suddenly developed a keen interest in the North Star.

Two days later, they reached the base of a towering mesa and Bear pointed at a notch in the base of it.

'That there's the trailhead. From there on, it's a steep climb for about a thousand feet and then we'll be at the eastern end of the valley. It's the only way

46

in and out, far as I know.'

Ben couldn't see the trail until they were right on top of it and Bear was right about its steepness. After a few hundred feet, they dismounted and led their string of horses up the precipitous, narrow slope. With frequent pauses to catch their breath in the thin, mountain air, they gradually made their way up to the valley entrance. Ben was wondering how many cattle had survived, when they passed through another notch and topped out.

The long, meandering valley lay before them and from where he sat, he counted at least a hundred head and there were probably many more around the bend of the valley floor. They looked to be in good shape, and there was a lot of young stuff.

Ben pointed to a place where the steep walls narrowed to less than a hundred feet and just a quarter mile from the trail they had just ascended. 'We'll build a fence and a gate across there to hold our gather.' Bear nodded.

For a week, they worked the brush and hills and made their muster. The herd had swelled to well over eight hundred head since Bear last saw them and they were in surprisingly good shape. Over half the herd was young stuff and breeding stock. They were wild and hard to hold, and Ben and Bear had their hands full. Finally, they figured they had as many as they were going to find, and decided to start the drive in the morning.

'We'll push them to the trailhead and they'll have

nowhere to go but down.' Ben sliced bacon into the pan while Bear made biscuits and stirred the beans. 'They may scatter some at the base of the mesa before we get down there ourselves, but they'll be easy to spot since it's fairly flat.'

Bear nodded and said, 'The hard part will be keepin' 'em together with just the two of us, but we'll make out.'

There was a chill in the air when they started the cattle heading toward the trail down the mesa the next morning. For a time, the lead cattle milled around at the trailhead, unwilling to descend, but gradually the pressure from the other cattle forced them down and the drive was underway. Ben and Bear whistled and shouted, waving their arms and urging the cattle forward. Finally, only Ben and Bear were left at the trailhead and then they too began making their way down. As Ben rounded a turn he could see the valley floor far below and saw that most of the cattle were already down and milling about.

Cattle, in spite of their clumsy appearance, are surprisingly sure-footed, and Ben didn't lose a single head on the steep descent. When they reached the base of the mesa, the bawling herd was still there, milling around and confused. They began pushing them east and gradually an old mossy-horn steer took the lead and the herd followed. They bedded down the first night after making about five miles. Ben considered that a fairly good start with a herd not yet broken to the trail and only two riders.

On the third day, they again spotted a party of Indians and Bear remarked that it looked like the same bunch they had seen on the way. Ben agreed and said, 'I'm going to ride over there and talk to them. Maybe we can help each other. You stay with the herd.'

There were two old men, two younger braves, one boy, two girls and two women. They watched Ben ride up. He spoke to them and learned they were migrating to a new camp. He could see that they had few belongings and even less food.

'I will bargain,' he said. 'I need two men to help me take my cattle to my valley. For this, I will pay well. What is your price?'

'Two horses and six cattle.' The speaker was the wounded brave Ben had once treated and who had subsequently helped Mattie. Neither occasion was mentioned.

'I am called Ben. What do they call you?'

'I am called Medicine Hawk. I will go with you and my son will go with you,' he said, tilting his head toward the boy.

'He can ride?' asked Ben.

'He can. He is young but he does a man's work.'

The boy looked to be about thirteen, and at that age, Ben had held down two jobs in Boston. Ben nodded. 'Very well, have your people cut out six cows from the herd. We can't spare any horses now but when we are through with the drive you shall have them.'

The cattle were now partially trail-broken and the drive was much easier. Both Medicine Hawk and his son proved to be good hands and they knew of the available water holes and grass. The cattle were in excellent shape and now seemed eager to see what was over the next hill.

They were within a day's ride of the valley when Hawk rode up to Ben and nodded at a column of dust approaching from the south. With his field glass, Ben could make out five, perhaps six riders. He turned and stood in his stirrups to find Bear and was gratified to see the old mountain man already peering toward the dust and looking to his rifle.

The riders drew up and studied the herd as Ben quietly rode up to them.

'I'm Daniel Goodwin,' said a big, pompous-looking blond man on a palomino, 'and I claim all unbranded cattle on this range.'

'Do you? Well, these cattle aren't from this range. We've driven them almost fifty miles and we intend to drive them further. You'd best stand aside. We want no trouble.'

'Boss, that there is Ben Tower, the man I told you about.'

Ben looked at the redheaded speaker. 'I know you. You'd be the man that tried to rob the Trail's End at Cook's Crossing. I see they failed to hang you.'

'That's right. I'm Dooley Clowers.'

'The Santa Fe gunman?'

50

'Some call me that. Them town people never bothered to lock that ice house door and my friends just lifted up the bolt one night and here I am.' He grinned. 'And as I remember, I owe you one.'

Goodwin pushed forward and stared at Ben. 'I don't care who you are or where you got these cows. This is my land and I'm claiming this here herd, so you just gather up your men and ride on out of here.'

Ben nudged his own horse forward and before anyone realized his intent, he was side by side with Goodwin's horse and the muzzle of his Winchester was planted firmly in the big man's belly.

'Now you listen to me. These are my cattle and I've worked hard to bring them all this way. I'm not about to give them up to you or anybody else.' There was hard steel in Ben's voice. 'Now I'm taking them on to the Rafter T. Will you give me passage, or do I need to blow your liver all over that saddle?'

Big Dan didn't like it. He didn't like it one bit, but the sharp front sight of Ben's rifle was buried in his gut and he knew Ben was not bluffing.

'You men turn around and ride on back the way we came,' he said over his shoulder.

'But boss . . .' began the protest.

'Do as I say!' he barked. 'Now move!'

Dooley Clowers pushed his horse forward, his face ugly and his hand on his gun butt.

'Damn you, Dooley! You'll get me killed. Now do as I say.'

51

Clowers glared at Ben for a moment and then wheeled his horse and moved off, cursing under his breath.

Goodwin turned back to Ben. 'This ain't over Tower, this ain't over by a long shot.'

'My ranch is the Rafter T, about a day's ride east of here. We call it the Rafter T Valley,' Ben said, 'and I never forget a face.'

'What's that supposed to mean?'

'It means that if I ever see your face, or one of these men on my range, I won't be asking questions. I'm going to figure that it's not a friendly visit and just start shooting.'

It was just after noon the next day when they pushed the herd on to the long, green grass of Rafter T Valley.

# 4

The time for the March thaw came and went without a sign of any warming trend. It had been a particularly harsh winter and Ben had been steadily losing stock to the bitter cold. There was plenty of feed beneath the thin crust of snow and the springs flowed despite below zero temperatures, but cattle, like all other creatures, can tolerate extremes just so long before succumbing and the gray overcast and strengthening westerly winds promised more to come.

Ben and Bear were checking waterholes when they came across the partially-eaten dead yearling. But unlike the others, this one had died from claw and fang and not the cold. The tracks told the tale as plainly as if it had been written in the snow. One particularly strange, peculiar track told yet another tale.

'That there's that big old grizzly from up yonder around the high timber.' Bear spat over his shoulder and wiped his chin, looking warily up the slope. 'From the looks of that track, he's done lost hisself a rear foot to a trap or somethin'. Crippled up like that, he'll be takin' a beef calf from now on when he wants some meat 'lessen he finds somethin' already dead.'

Ben nodded up at the trail. 'We'd best follow his tracks and put him down while we have a trail to follow. He'll be a menace otherwise and besides, I'll see no creature suffer like that anyway, not even a bear. He's fed up on meat and headed back up the slope, probably to den up somewhere. I'll follow him from here and you go back to the ranch-house and get us supplies for about a week. Ride on up to the overlook and wait. I can see that outcropping from most anywhere and I'll keep an eye out for you.'

He glanced at the graying sky. 'Maybe this weather will hold off for a time. Then again, maybe not.'

The first flakes of snow were falling when Ben got down to spell his horse. There was a blizzard building, sure enough, and he needed to locate shelter soon and build a fire. A little worried now, he hoped Bear would see the snow on the mountain and wait it out before packing supplies up as they had discussed. But it was no real concern. Bear was more than able to take care of himself.

Ben was nearly seven-thousand feet up and the freshening wind was peppering the cold snow against his exposed face. He had just turned to dig a bandanna out of his saddle-bags when something slammed into his back with terrific force. The horse bolted, and he flipped off backward, smashing his head violently against a rock. He tried to rise but fell on his face and then the world faded from gray to utter blackness. For a long time, he knew nothing.

'You ain't dead?' The unfamiliar cold voice brought him to his senses and with great effort he rolled over onto his back. The man sitting his horse and looking at him was a stranger.

'I thought I'd killed you. Took me almost an hour to get off that ridge to see if you was dead.'

The strangely flat and emotionless voice had a vaguely familiar ring as did the gray, hooded eyes that studied him quietly.

'Who are you? Why'd you shoot me?'

'It don't matter none. All that matters is that you die and stay dead.' The stranger eased his pistol out of his waistband and calmly fired into Ben once and then again. He watched the blood begin to flow from Ben's head and chest and noted the half-lidded eyes gazing at the leaden sky but seeing nothing. Satisfied, he turned and started down the mountain. The snow began to fall faster, and the sound of the wind became more urgent.

For a long time, Ben lay still, halfway between life and death. Then the bitter cold overcame even the shock of his wounds and his mind staggered back to consciousness. For a moment he couldn't remember where he was or what had happened. Then the memory of the cold-blooded shooting came back to him.

Slowly he began to assess his situation. His horse was nowhere in sight and he was partially covered in the snow that was now coming down hard. The wind had increased, and drifts were beginning to build. He could see no more than fifty feet. He was in desperate trouble.

Groaning, he forced himself to try to rise. On the third attempt, he managed to roll over on his face. He got his hands under him and finally pushed himself to his knees. For a while he paused, laboring to catch his breath. He must find shelter and must find it soon. He tried to rise but failed. He began to crawl.

Twice he fainted. Both times, cold snow melting on his face brought him around and he pushed on. He vaguely remembered an outcropping somewhere off to his left and maybe a mile distant. It might be made into a rough shelter and there was fuel there from a lightning-felled oak. But with only a few feet of visibility, there was a good chance that he would miss it entirely. He had to chance it. It was all he had.

Amazingly, there were apparently no bones broken and no vital organs hit but he had lost a lot of blood. His probing fingers told him that the bullet to his head had cut a furrow along his scalp that had bled a great deal but was not serious. The bitter cold was his enemy now, but it was also partly responsible for stopping the bleeding. Once, while he rested, he checked his pockets and found his tin of matches and a strong pocket-knife. His rifle was still on the saddle and his holster was empty, so his revolver was probably lying somewhere under the snow. He also found a sandwich that was to have been his lunch. Now it was a matter of life or death. A man must have food to survive the cold.

He crawled as far as he could go. Finally, his knees and hands became so scraped and bloody that he was unable to crawl any farther. He must either get to his feet or die. He picked up a stout limb to use as a walking stick and put one end on the ground in front of him. Using both hands, he began to pull himself to his feet. Straining with desperation, he finally gained his feet and stood unsteadily in the gale-force wind, but he stood nonetheless. Keeping a firm grip on the stick, he took first one step and then another.

He lost track of the times he fell on the icy slope but each time willed himself back on his feet. He forced himself to remember the cold, gray eyes and the flat, merciless voice. He forced himself to remember the cold-blooded shooting and leaving him for dead. He used this memory to create the heat and determination of righteous anger that gave him the strength and will to overcome his desperate situation. The visibility was now less than ten feet in the wind-driven blizzard. He pushed on.

Finally, totally exhausted, he sat on a flat shelf of

rock and faced the fact that he had gone as far as he could go. After a long time, he raised his head and looked wearily around. As he did, the snow eased up a bit and he could see that the rock he was sitting on was part of a large outcropping and above his head was the lighting-struck oak. He had made it.

Under a narrow shelf jutting out from the face of the outcropping, he gathered stones for a low wall and to serve as a reflector for his fire. He leaned several poles against the shelf at the top and the wall at the bottom and laced as many sticks as he could horizontally to serve as a crude windbreak and hoped that the snow might fill in some of the openings. It wasn't much of a shelter, but it would have to do.

He found some bark and dry twigs beneath a sheltering rock and began to construct a pile of fuel for his fire. Using first dry twigs and then larger pieces, he built a teepee shape over his kindling. Before he lit it, he looked around for larger logs to bank his fire and to eventually burn. He spied a good-sized piece sticking out from near the wall and went to retrieve it. That act saved his life. He stumbled onto the almost-hidden entrance of a small cave.

The walls and ceiling were blackened with the soot of ancient fires and above, he could dimly make out daylight shining down through some cleft in the rock forming a natural chimney. His fuel, transferred into the cave, blazed brightly, and for the first time in hours, he began to feel some warmth creeping back into his bones. As he sat and ate his sandwich, he looked around the rest of the small room. In the rear of the cave was a good-sized pile of dry wood, placed there by someone who had used the shelter long ago. There was also a pile of leaves, more than a little fur, and the strong, musky odor of bear.

Bear had just reached the ranch and was explaining the situation when he and Mattie heard the faint report of a gunshot far up the western slope.

'Maybe he got the bear,' Mattie said.

'Don't think so. That there was a pistol shot. He wouldn't shoot no bear with a pistol, 'lessen he was jumped and had no time to get out his rifle.'

Later, Mattie handed Bear the sacks of food and then stepped out of the barn and gazed up the mountain through the steady snowfall. She could see nothing, nor did she expect to. Then she heard two more closely-spaced gunshots.

'Heard 'em.' Bear was mounted and had the pack-horse in tow. 'Maybe he took on that bear with a hand weapon after all. Maybe not. I'll be leavin' now.'

'Be careful, Bear. It's shaping up for a blizzard.'

Soon after, Bear came upon Ben's horse walking slowly toward the ranch and trailing its reins. Blood splashes showed on the saddle, but the horse was unharmed, so it was not likely a bear attack. The horse was tired and skittish, but Bear would need him when he found Ben, so he added it to his string. He headed up the mountain. The wind subsided but the snow fell steadily. The creaking saddle and constant beat of the hoofs were muffled in the hushed silence of falling snow. Mattie was right about the blizzard, but Bear's real worry was what had happened to Ben.

Ben dug through his pockets again and pulled out his tin coffee cup. Filling it with fresh snow, he settled it in the coals. Later, he dropped some grounds from another pocket into the hot water. The coffee tasted good. The cave was relatively warm and so was he.

Filling the cup again, he opened his coat and shirt and bathed his wounds with the hot water. The first shot had hit low in his back and had gone through without touching anything vital as far as he could tell. The chest shot had hit the tally book in his shirt pocket and stopped just under the skin. Using his knife, he popped it out and plugged the hole with wadded cloth cut from his shirt. He was sore and weak from loss of blood and shock, but perhaps he was not seriously injured after all. His head ached fiercely from both the gunshot wound and the blow from his fall on the rock, but those too, did not seem to be serious.

He would stay the night and head back to the ranch in the morning, if he was able. He pulled his coat back on and settled in. Outside, the wind fell silent, but the snow continued to fall. Ben fed the fire and then stretched out beside it. In minutes, he was asleep.

The first blow threw him against the far wall of the cave and he instantly felt a rib break. Somewhere, blood began flowing as he scrambled for what little cover he could find. With a deafening roar in the tiny space, the bear charged, crushing him against the wall. Again, he was slapped aside and then he felt giant jaws clamping down on the calf of his right leg. In desperation, he grabbed a glowing stick from the fire and jabbed it where he thought the bear's eyes must be. With an agonized scream, the bear dropped Ben's leg and began to roll and thrash violently about, digging at its eyes and tossing scattering rocks, dirt, and firewood in all directions. Ben grabbed another burning stick and crept to the farthest corner.

The bear suddenly stopped his rampage and sat in the semi-darkness, rocking back and forth and whining in pain, mewling and bawling softly. Even in his own great pain and imminent danger, Ben felt pity for him. He moved slightly to his left to ease off a sharp point and accidentally dislodged a rock which fell beside him. With a savage roar the bear charged the sound and the last thing Ben remembered was a violent blow to the side of his head, the raking of huge claws, and a tremendous, roaring explosion.

*

The face was that of a stranger, but it was a kind-looking face. Ben recognized the surroundings as his own bedroom, but he was too weak to ask the stranger his business. He looked to his left and saw a tearful Mattie, wringing her hands. It occurred to him that he'd never seen her openly crying, not even when she'd lost her entire family.

'Well son, looks like you've had a rough go of it but you're in remarkably good shape, save for that leg. I'm going to put a poultice on it to draw out the infection and then we shall see. Mind you, a bear bite often turns gangrenous, what with all the rotten meat they find, so chances are that we may have to take the leg. Just so you know.'

He stopped and smiled at Ben. 'I guess I should have introduced myself. I'm Matthew Ridgeway, the new doctor from Cook's Crossing. Bear fetched me after he brought you home.'

Ben turned to Mattie. 'How long?' he whispered.

'You mean how long have you been here?'

Ben nodded.

'Four days, not counting the full day it took Bear to get you here on a travois.'

'I'll be on my way,' said the doctor, picking up his bag. He glanced sharply at Mattie. 'Looks like you'll be having that baby in a month or so. Will you be having a woman to help you or will you be requiring my services?'

'I'll send for you when the time comes, and thank you, Doctor Ridgeway.'

'You was in some fight!' Bear entered the room. 'That bear was blinded in the right eye for sure and probably couldn't see much out of the left one neither. I was trackin' him and spotted a bloody hand print on a saplin' before I realized we was both trackin' you! Good thing I heard him screamin' when you jobbed him with that firebrand or I might have missed that cave openin'. As it was, I had to shoot from outside 'cause that cave was too full of grizzly, you, and fightin' for me to get in. He only had three paws like I thought. His left rear must have been lost to a trap. I ain't partial to traps. Don't mind huntin' but never liked to see a critter suffer.'

Bear turned to go. He looked back and asked, 'Know who shot you?'

Ben shook his head. 'Never saw him before,' he whispered, 'but he looked familiar somehow. I reckon he thinks I'm dead.'

Despite the poultice, Ben's leg began to fester and was hot to the touch. Mattie sent for Medicine Hawk who lifted the sheets and smelled the wound. He left without a word and returned hours later with a foul-smelling black concoction which he smeared liberally on Ben's injury. By the next morning, the wound felt better and cooler to the touch. The following day, Mattie found Ben standing unsteadily at the window, gazing at the work going on without him.

'You're supposed to be resting in bed.'

'Spring roundup won't wait, Mattie. We've lost

stock and we need to make a gather, so we can see where we are.'

'I know. I told the doctor you'd do your healing in the saddle.'

Ben turned and looked down at her. 'What'd he say to that?'

'He just shook his head and left.'

## 5

Ben tied the big gray to the rail and slapped some of the dust off his clothes with his hat. The territorial capital was somewhat larger than he had imagined, but a gold strike can grow a fair-sized city almost overnight. He'd already taken care of his business with the Territorial Governor's office, so he thought he'd best catch up on the latest news at the Cattleman's Saloon before finding a room. The streets were all but deserted and the town was quiet in the heat of late afternoon. He paused at the batwing doors and surveyed the cool, dark interior before entering, a habit held over from his days as a Boston tough.

Ben ordered a drink and listened quietly to the

conversations about Indians, cattle prices, and range conditions. To his left, a friendly, political dispute went on and on with no possibility of resolution.

'You're Ben Tower, ain'tcha?' The speaker was dressed in greasy buckskins with fringe sewn into the sleeves and legs to help shed rainwater. A Sharps .50 rested on the wall behind him and one of the new Bowie-style knives was in his waistband. At the sound of Ben's name, a tall man standing at the far end of the bar stiffened, turned slowly, gaped wide-eyed at Ben for a moment and then left quietly and unnoticed out the back way.

'Well if it isn't Clay Johnson, from up Montana way.' Ben grinned. 'What are you doing down here, you old skinner? The buffalo are all gone around these parts!'

'Market's gone too. Can't get nothin' fer skins nor tongues no more. Ain't no call fer 'em what with beef bein' so cheap and plentiful. But the buffs are almost all hunted out anyways. Ain't seen a decent-sized herd in months.'

Clay paused to light his pipe. He glanced up at Ben. 'Know anybody who can use a hand? I'm still a good teamster and a fair hand with a rope.'

'I got a spread south of here that could use a few good hands. Get your gear and we'll ride out in the morning. Have you had your supper yet?'

'Tell the truth, I ain't et in a couple of days.' He looked down at the floor, shamefaced. 'I got no money, Ben. I'm flat broke.'

'Actually, you do have some money. Remember that load of skins we went halves on and then I bought you out? Well, the market was higher than we thought, and I owe you forty dollars.' Ben took out his wallet and peeled off the cash.

'You're a damn liar, Ben, but I thank you fer not shamin' me.'

'I'll see you at the Emporium dining hall for supper as soon as I get a room and wash up.'

The waitress was a freckled redhead with a light-hearted way about her. At the next table, a rowdy, young cowhand watched her every move, with lovesick eyes, all the while trying to appear disinterested. The redhead was obviously enjoying every minute of it.

'What'll it be, gentlemen? We have beef stew and fried chicken tonight.'

They ordered, and Ben gave her a smile as she walked away.

'Don't get no ideas, mister. That there's to be my girl.'

Ben looked over at the cowhand and nodded. 'I'm sure she is, son. I have no interest in her. Just being friendly.'

'She ain't good enough for you?'

Ben realized that the young man was drunk. 'I meant nothing by that, son. I'm not looking for trouble.'

'Well I ain't your son and it looks like you got trouble.'

The young man started to rise so Ben hooked a toe around the leg of his chair and jerked hard, tumbling the cowhand to the floor. Ben rose and, appearing to kneel beside his victim, drove his right knee into the kid's chest, knocking the wind out of him.

'Looks like you've had a bit too much to drink, son,' Ben said aloud to the gasping cowhand. 'Maybe you'd better go sleep it off.'

He bent over and said quietly, 'Best let it go, boy. I could just as easily have killed you, and many men would have done just that. You're not the tough *hombre* you think you are, so don't pick fights, especially when you're pie-eyed drunk. Besides, that girl likes you just fine! Can't you see that?'

The cowhand stumbled from the room and the men finished their dinner. The stone-faced redhead brought their check, dropped it on the table without a word, and stalked off without looking at them. Ben grinned and paid the tab.

The night air was cool and had a promising smell of rain. In the far distance, clouds lit up like ghostly lanterns as silent lightning weaved its way through their misty interiors. Somewhere a door slammed, and somebody splashed a bucket of water into the street. In one of the saloons, a rinky-tink piano hammered out a tune.

Clay Johnson lit his pipe and nodded down the street. 'Got me a bed at the roomin' house yonder fer the night. I'll see you at the livery in the morning.'

The street was dimly lit from lights in the various saloons and restaurants as Ben strolled to the Emporium. As he descended the boardwalk's steps to cross the street, his pant leg snagged on a splinter. He bent to free it and a shot bullet slammed into the rail over his head. As he dove to his left, he heard a second shot and saw a muzzle flash coming from between two buildings across the street and a shadowy figure. Instantly he fired, rolled twice and fired again. A man lurched from the gloom and sagged slowly to the ground.

Ben heard running steps behind him and whirled. It was Clay.

'Heard shots and come a-runnin'. Figgered that damn fool kid must'a been layin' fer you. Did you see who it was?'

'That's him lying in the street over there. Could be that kid I suppose. Let's go see.'

Ben heard moaning as he approached. He reached down, picked up the man's gun and then rolled him over. Instantly he recognized the cold, gray eyes staring up at him. It was the man who had shot him and left him for dead last month.

'Who are you and why are you gunning for me?'

'I'm paid to kill you. Twice paid,' he groaned.

'Who would pay to kill me?'

'Jack Stanton.'

*Jack Stanton!* The leader of the old Boston gang and father of the man he had killed with his own knife. Jack Stanton, after all this time and distance!

'You said you were paid twice.'

'Dunno who the other feller was. He heard I was askin' after you so he sent a man who told me where I could find you and gave me hundred dollars to see to it you was dead. I thought you was killed sure. I shot you three times.'

'Guess you were wrong. Now who are you? You look familiar somehow.'

'Dave Stanton, Jacks's brother.' He closed his eyes and grimaced in pain.

Ben stood back and watched as the local doctor looked Stanton over. After a while, the doctor rose and shook his head. 'He's gone. Two bullets square to the chest. Wonder he lasted this long.'

He glanced at Ben. 'Saw it from up there.' He nodded at a balcony above them. 'My office balcony. I was getting some night air. He ambushed you plain and clear. Someone you knew?'

'I didn't know him. Didn't know him at all.'

Mattie was picking tomatoes when she felt the first cramp. It passed quickly enough but she knew from helping her mid-wife mother that it was probably her time. Using her gathered apron as a basket, she finished picking her tomatoes and made her way back to the cabin. In the valley below, the sound of distant hammers and saws echoed as the carpenters worked steadily on raising the house and outbuildings. The new barn stood proud and strong with its coat of red paint and white trim, and the corral was already in use as young horses were being broken to ways of man.

Bear looked up from some tack he was repairing as Mattie approached the cabin porch. Something about her awkward bearing raised an alarm.

'You under the weather, Mattie?'

'Fetch Doc Ridgeway from town, would you, Bear?'

'Why sure, but what should I tell him?'

Mattie gave Bear her cool, level gaze. 'Just fetch him, Bear. He'll know why.'

Bear's neck and ears grew red and hot. 'Yes'm. I'll fetch him right away.'

Bear broke into a shambling run and Mattie laughed in spite of herself. It was the first time she'd ever seen the old man move any faster than he had to. She sat in her rocking chair in the cool shade of the porch and moments later heard Bear headed for town at a full gallop.

'Don't kill your horse for pity's sake,' she mumbled. As if he heard her, Bear slowed his mount to a more reasonable gait. Mattie sighed and braced herself as she felt another cramp coming on. Far to the north, a spring storm muttered and rumbled. She wondered when Ben would come home.

Ben and Clay made camp for the night under a shelf of rock hidden behind a stand of aspens. A faint trail had been followed on a hunch and led to both the shelter and good grass for the horses. The curly-headed Clay had proved to be a good hand and an even better cook. Ben already had plans to replace Digger Jones with Clay as ranch cook as soon as they reached the Rafter T. Digger hated the job, but he was better at it than the other hands, so he was stuck with the cooking. Clay Johnson would be a welcome change all around.

Clay pushed the coffee pot closer to their small, almost hidden fire. To the south and west, thunder grumbled, and the air carried a faint scent of rain. Already, a freshening wind had the aspens rustling, and lightning danced on the horizon, though still miles away. The hot coffee tasted good and warmed them against the chill.

'Think it'll hit here, boss?'

'Probably. We'd best gather the horses and stretch a rope under this shelf to tie off the reins. They might pull those picket pins if that lighting gets too close.'

'Yup, and lightin'll kill a horse sure as anythin'. I seen it once up north. Kilt a string of six, quick as a blink.'

Hours later, the rain began, a steady, ground-soaking rain that promised to go on all night. Far above, thunder cracked and rolled across the leaden sky. Ben edged his bedroll farther under the shelf. He slept.

A pebble bounced off Ben's bedroll. 'I hear them,' he whispered.

The men listened to the sound of hoofs on the

main trail below. It was early morning and the rain
had stopped. Only water dripping from the aspens
and the rock overhang disturbed the damp stillness.
The riders stopped somewhere below to rest their
horses and Clay and Ben moved quietly to their own
horses and held their nostrils for silence.

'I heard tell that the folks who saw it said that
there Tower is hell on wheels with a gun.' The voice
was clear in the cool air following the rain.

'He put two slugs in that Stanton feller's chest you
could'a covered with a poker chip and he done it
while he was rollin' on the ground.'

Another voice spoke up. 'All I know is the man
wants Tower dead and he's willing to pay five
hundred dollars to the hombre who does it, and he
ain't particular about how it's done, so I'll be layin'
for him.'

After another moment's rest, the riders moved
on.

A few miles to the northwest, lightning flashed,
and heavy sheets of rain darkened the morning sky.
Ben was reluctant to leave their shelter, but he
needed to trail the riders and perhaps discover who
was willing to pay big money for his death, so they
broke camp and rode down the slope to the main
trail. The muddy tracks told them there were three
riders, all big men riding big horses.

Topping a rise, they spotted the riders far below,
perhaps two miles away and about to ford a narrow
stream with a rocky bed and steep banks. As they

watched, the cowboys entered the swift stream and slowly began picking their way through the muddy waters in treacherous footing.

'Boss! Would you look at that!'

Around a bend in the stream and unseen by the crossing riders scarcely fifty yards away, a massive wall of water laden with tumbling logs, boulders, and debris was swiftly bearing down on the unsuspecting cowhands. Ben reached for his pistol to fire a warning shot but just then the crashing roar of the flash flood reached the riders below. As a man, they turned and stared at the churning mass of water and then in panicked desperation, threw caution to the wind and spurred their mounts across the slippery streambed of worn and rounded rocks. One rider went down immediately, his horse screaming in terror. For a moment, the remaining two looked like they might make it but then the huge wave caught them, and they vanished beneath its fury. Ben looked on in horror as the wave roared around another bend downstream, leaving a rolling torrent of muddy death in its wake.

For a moment, Ben and Clay sat in shock.

'That flood came from that storm yonder.' Clay nodded at the black clouds on their right. 'I've seen sudden flash floods come up in areas where the sun is shining bright, from a storm far over on the horizon.'

Ben shook his head sadly. 'Those poor devils.'

'They was plannin' on killin' you.' Clay glanced

sharply at Ben and then leaned over and spat on the ground.

'I'll fight and I'll kill if need be, but I'll wish that manner of death on no man.' Ben jerked his head toward their back trail. 'We may as well head back to that rock shelf and make camp again. That storm is moving our way and it'll be at least tomorrow before that water recedes enough to make a crossing.'

In fact, it was two days before they could ford the stream and it was chancy at that. The horses stumbled and struggled to maintain their footing and both riders had to resort to the spurs more than once to keep them moving. At last they gained the far side and mounted the steep banks, clouds of steam rising from their horses. They pulled up to let them blow.

'Look over there, boss.'

Clay pointed to a pile of brush and rocks jammed between the trunks of two giant cottonwood trees. It took Ben a moment to locate the boot and leg protruding from under a medium-sized boulder.

'Do you know him?'

It had taken them almost two hours of prying out limbs and rock to recover the body.

'Yeah, reckon I do. He was a hard-case who hung around the Cattleman's. Fact is, he was there the day I run into you.' Clay paused and lit his pipe. 'Come to think of it, he disappeared right after! Think he might'a been the one who tipped off that Stanton feller?'

'Could be. Let's get out the shovels and bury him.'

'You do beat all. He would have left you fer the buzzards.'

Ben glanced at Clay. 'Would you have just left him?'

Clay gestured with his pipe stem. 'See that knoll yonder under the oak? That's where I figgered to plant him if you didn't.'

## 6

'Well hell, I thought you was dead and ate by the hogs.' Bear eyed Clay, spat over his shoulder and wiped his beard with a sleeve.

Clay grinned in reply. 'And I thought you was long ago hung fer stealin' sheep!'

'I take it you boys know each other,' Ben said dryly, gazing down the slopes at the tall, green grasses of the Rafter T. Far below, the hands were building a fence to keep cattle out of the ranch-house yard. The new buildings were up, and the roofs were on.

'OK, give me the news, Bear.'

'Dooley Clowers is gone. He showed up in Cook's Crossin' and called out that saloon keeper, Jacob Talley. Figgered on shootin' him down in the street for jailin' him that time he tried to hold up the saloon, or so he bragged. But old Talley come through them half-doors with a scatter gun and backed Dooley down. Dooley mounted up and we ain't seen him since. Folks step pretty easy around old man Talley these days.

'How's Mattie?'

'Oh well, Mattie's fine, just fine. So's the rest of the family.'

'Family? What family?'

'Why your family,' Bear said innocently. 'What family do ya suppose I mean?'

'What are you blathering on about?'

'You're a father, that's what!'

'Holy smoke! I am? How's Mattie? Boy or girl?'

'Yup, she's fine, just like I said, and boys.'

'She's fine? That's great news! I've been some worried with me gone and all and . . . wait . . . what? What did you say? *Boys*? What do you mean, *boys*?'

'Yessir,' Bear said, enjoying every minute of it, 'Yessir, I said boys. Two of 'em just alike and as ornery as any I've ever saw. Why they squalled all night long last night and we could hear 'em clear out in the bunkhouse. You're in for some real ear music from them two!'

Mattie laughed when she told Ben of Bear's frantic ride to fetch Doc Ridgeway and her own shock of discovering she was carrying identical twin boys. She was supposed to have been bedridden for two weeks, but after one day, she got up and felt fine. That was over a week ago.

'Who is who, Mattie?' asked Ben, looking down at his sons. 'What're their names?'

'That's up to you, Ben. They're your sons. You

name them.'

Ben stood up and looked over at Mattie. 'How about we call the one with that little birthmark on his back, Joseph, and the other one, Jeremiah?'

Mattie nodded.

'Old Pete thinks he may have hit a very rich vein, Ben.' Mattie placed a plate full of beef and potatoes in front of Ben. She sat in her rocker and began nursing Joseph. She looked up. 'I think he's a little worried that you may change your arrangement with him.'

'A bargain is a bargain, Mattie. We agreed that we would go halves on anything he found prospecting around the ranch. I gave him my word, and in the west, a man's word is worth more than any amount of gold. I'll talk to him.'

'I know that, Ben, and I already told Pete, but he'll want to hear it from you.'

'The food's good, Mattie, which reminds me – I hired us a ranch cook. His name is Clay Johnson. I knew him up in Montana years back and he rode in with me. He'll replace Digger Jones, who never much cottoned to the job anyway.'

'He isn't very good at it either,' Mattie said drily. 'Why not have your Mr Clay Johnson take over the cooking chore here in the main house and feed everyone here at our table? Digger's been feeding the crew and I've been cooking here in the house.'

'You sure?'

'Yes. We've a large table and lots of chairs coming next week and the dining room is plenty big. Let the hands eat in here from now on.' She lifted her eyes to him. 'Treat them like family, Ben, and they'll be loyal like family.'

Pete Nagle's find was a good one. He'd panned a small creek that wound its way along the eastern slope for some eight miles, and had suddenly found good color and then, just as abruptly, he had lost it. The gold was rough-textured and hadn't been subjected to the polishing and rounding off that came from tumbling for miles in a rocky creek bed. He filled his pipe and found a good stump from which he studied the mountainside.

Pete had stopped by the ranch-house last fall hoping for a feed and hadn't been disappointed. After supper, the conversation turned to prospecting, old Pete's favorite topic. Ben asked several questions and then, satisfied that Pete knew mining, made a proposal.

'We've found some color along the eastern slope of the Rafter T and I'm guessing there's more, possibly much more. I'll go halves with you on any strike you find, and I'll bring in the equipment and men as needed.'

Pete glanced sharply at Ben.

'You'll go halves with me? I've never been offered no halves before. Best I ever got was thirds and I had to get it out myself.'

'Gold's worth nothing if it lies undiscovered in the ground, and right now Pete, I have one hundred percent of nothing. I'd rather have fifty percent of a fortune. I have a feeling that it's there, but I don't know where to look. You do. Do we have a deal?'

In the west, bargains worth a fortune were often sealed with no more than a handshake, and Pete Nagle rode out the next morning with an extra pack-horse and a month's supply of grub and equipment. There would be a line rider along now and then to check on him and bring new supplies. He made permanent camp under some aspens and went to work.

Patience is the name of the game in prospecting. Pete worked out the probable spots in the creek bed where gold would be likely to settle and began to test for color. Filling the pan with dirt, gravel, and water, he worked the gold to the bottom by keeping all the solids suspended in the water using a constant to-and-fro swirling motion. After a minute or two, the lighter materials worked their way to the top and he carefully washed that layer out of the pan by a back and forth movement under the water. Then he resumed the to-and-fro swirling action to further settle the gold and raise the lighter stuff. After a few cycles of this, he was down to the remaining heavy, black sands and hopefully, the gold.

It was during one of these tests that Pete suddenly had a pan with almost an ounce of coarse, yellow flakes and small nuggets. As he worked his way upstream, each succeeding pan netted new color and one had almost two ounces, an incredibly rich find. Then, just as suddenly as it began, the gold petered out. Several more test pans yielded only an occasional small flake or two.

Seated on the stump, Pete spotted several outcroppings that might have been the source of the jagged gold, but he was not convinced. One by one, he inspected and discarded them until all had been eliminated. Puzzled, he began walking the slope on a diagonal, back and forth for over a mile wide looking for any sign of the source and found nothing. For three weeks he traversed the slopes, steadily to and fro looking for anything, any clue. Nothing.He knew two things. The source was not far away, and it had only fairly recently begun to find its way to the stream. If it had been eroding for centuries, the gold would have worked its way far down the stream bed and closer to the bedrock. Instead, it had mostly been found quite near the surface and had traveled only a short distance downstream.

Pete moved his camp to save walking time, and built a lean-to against a fallen, giant fir, long ago downed by lightning, and about a third of the way up the slope. It offered a good view of the valley and of the creek below, and boughs woven in the branches offered shelter for his mule and packhorse from the spring rains.

It was the morning after one of those rains when he walked to where the downed fir's giant roots stood upturned and stark against the sky. As he yawned, he gazed down into the deep hole, where a yellow gleam, wet from the rains caught his eye. With a growing excitement, he scrambled down and picked the object up. Wiping the mud off with his shirtsleeve, he stared at a rough, jagged, and stunningly beautiful piece of gold that must have weighed six ounces or better. The ground beneath the roots was littered with dark, rotten quartz. He examined the roots themselves and found several more pieces of gold among the rocks and dirt, still imbedded in the tangle. He had found the source.

When Ben rode up, the mine was already nearly fifteen feet in, twenty feet wide and growing. The outer limits of the vein were not yet established, and it had already proved to be fabulously rich. Pete gave orders on some shoring placement and walked out to greet Ben.

'I hear you've made quite a strike, and I also hear that you think I may not be a man of my word.'

Pete's neck and ears grew bright red and he studied his boots for a moment before answering.

'Aw, it ain't that so much, boss. It's just that I've seen brothers kill each other over less than this. I ain't doubting you, but men do change their minds when there's riches like this involved. I've seen it and I guess I was a little worried.'

Ben decided to let him off the hook. 'I know it, Pete. Men have been killed over five dollars in a poker game and after all, you don't really know me, so I'll take no offense. The deal stands. I now have half a bonanza. I'd call that a pretty fair deal for any man.'

The two men discussed the need for more shoring timbers, blasting powder, food and shelter, and a stamp mill. When the talk got around to hiring some guards, Pete indicated a small hill to the west and about two miles off. 'Someone's been watching us. I'd seen the sun flashing off a spyglass of a morning when the sun's right, so I had a rider mosey off to the north and sorta circle around to the far side of that there hill. He found the tracks of one horse and where a man's boot heels had dug in behind a dead-fall and plenty of them Mexican-style cigarette stubs laying around. From his position, he had a good view of the mine workings. On the far side of the hill, he had him a camp hid in some rocks where the fire could not be seen. From the sign, he had been there most of a week. Maybe the rider spooked him off.'

Ben found the tracks himself and trailed them until they were covered by more recent cattle tracks, which then led into the soft sands of the river. He cast back and forth for over two hours but was unable to find where the rider had gone. He cata-logued and saved the track to memory as was the way of cattlemen. If he saw it again, he would instantly recognize it.

It was late afternoon when he topped the hill south of the Rafter T and looked down on his home. The long, low main house with its covered porch and huge, shady, cottonwoods was flanked on the south by the big barn. In the barnyard, he could make out a dozen or so of Mattie's chickens, idly scratching in the dust for food and grit. To the west, the bunkhouse and stables were also nestled among giant cottonwoods. Farther north was the original cabin, now used as a storehouse.

To the west, the valley and slopes were dotted with cattle. In the spring, he would round up some of the older stuff and begin a drive east to the rail yards and cattle buyers. The timber-cutting on the west slopes was ongoing but the careful selection had left the hillside mostly intact. He had seen what happens when hills are stripped of trees, and wanted no part of it. One town had been buried under a mudslide after the hills above it were laid bare, cutting ties and bridge timbers for the railroad.

Standing in his stirrups, Ben looked all the way around. As far as he could see, everything belonged to the Rafter T, nearly three hundred square miles and close to two hundred thousand acres, and if all went as planned, it would soon more than double that. It was a big land and he had big plans for it. And it would take a big man to hold it.

# 7

It was hot and dusty work. Ben gave his mount a breather on a low rise and watched as two of the hands hazed steers out of the lower breaks. To his right and below, were the branding fires with a steady stream of roped and bawling calves calling to nervous mothers. The air was filled with the stench of burning hair mingled with wood smoke as the red-hot Rafter T irons did their work. One by one the calves were branded and released to scamper back to their waiting mothers, wide-eyed and frightened but none the worse for their brief ordeal. Within minutes, all was forgotten, and they returned to peaceful grazing.

The spring roundup was nearly complete and there was a sizable herd of prime beef ready to be driven east to the rail yards. With ample young stuff and good breeding stock, the ranch herd had grown to one of the largest in the country and it was time to market the older stock.

Half a mile to the south, Bear suddenly pulled up and studied the ground intently for a moment and then looked off to the south and the riverbank. He turned in the saddle, waved his hat at Ben, and headed off. Ben kneed his own mount and turned to follow, wondering what Bear had spotted. In less than two hundred yards, he cut a strange trail and after no more than a glance, he understood Bear's intent. Two more hands had cut the trail and the party grew to four by the time they rounded a bend in the river and rode into the stranger's campsite.

'Light and set, gents. Coffee's hot.' Seated by the fire under a huge cottonwood was one of the largest men Ben had ever seen. His massive arms and chest stretched the denim shirt tautly over rippling muscles. His huge, blond head was set on a thick neck above an open collar bristling with curly, red, chest hair. He got to his feet with a grace rare for a man his size and stood inches over Ben's own impressive height and outweighed him by thirty pounds, all of it hard muscle.

'Just rode in from Texas. Been near four months on the trail.' The big man grinned at the unsmiling group studying him from horseback.

'You're a liar,' said Ben.

The grin remained, but the eyes hardened. 'Now that ain't a real friendly way to say howdy to a stranger, mister.'

'It wasn't meant friendly. Like I said, you're a liar.'

The rifle held in the crook of Bear's arms was now pointed casually in the big stranger's general direction, a fact that everyone noticed, including the stranger.

'Drop that gun-belt, and be right careful about it,' Ben ordered.

Slowly the man complied, the grin fading to a frown.

'Is this the way you treat newcomers in this territory?'

'You're no newcomer. You've been watching my mine diggings for months. All of us have seen the tracks of that horse of yours many times, and the boot prints around your fire there are almost as familiar as my own. And I see you're still smoking those Mexican-style cigarettes. No, sir, you're not new here at all.'

'You talk real tough when you have a man disarmed and outnumbered.' The big man glanced around and spat in Ben's direction.

Ben unbuckled his gun-belt and handed it to Bear. 'Hold this.'

Startled, Bear threw a hard glance at Ben. 'What the hell are you doin'?'

The big man watched in astonishment as Ben swung down, the disbelief on his face soon replaced by the return of the grin. 'You'd fight *me*?'

'No, I'm not going to fight you. I'm going to whip you good. There won't be any fight to it. What's your name anyway?'

'It's Cab Renfro, a name you'll not soon forget!' Renfro spat into each big fist and wiped them on his jeans. He watched Ben and waited, fists moving slightly in anticipation.

As a young tough in Boston, Ben had once jostled a smaller, young man of obvious means who was well-dressed and looked to be quite the dandy. The stranger had apologized, and Ben took it as a sign of fear, so he decided to rawhide him. One thing led to another and Ben took a swing. The jaw he was aiming at was suddenly somewhere else and the little dandy caught him with two vicious left jabs followed by a straight right that jarred Ben all the way to his heels. That went on until the untouched stranger asked a bleeding Ben if he'd had enough. Ben thought about it for a moment, realized he'd been thoroughly whipped and offered his hand with a grin.

As so often happens with men, the one-time foes quickly became good friends and the dandy turned out to be none other than Ian Dawson, a lightweight prizefighter from Scotland, and in Boston for several lucrative matches. He took Ben on as a sparring partner and taught him the science of boxing.

After a few months, Ben's superior size, reach, and strength, coupled with his new skills and natural talent made him more than a match for Ian, so he proposed that Ben try his hand in the ring in his proper weight class. He lost his first bout but won all the rest. He was well on his way to a career in boxing when he killed gangster Jack Stanton's son with his own knife and left Boston in a hurry.

Ben walked up to Renfro and slapped him hard across his grinning mouth with the back of his left hand, instantly bloodying both lips. Shocked and then enraged, Renfro charged, throwing a great looping overhand right at Ben's head. Ben stepped to his own right, nonchalantly slapped away the blow with his left and hit Renfro square on the jaw with a straight right. Renfro's eyes glazed over for a moment, but he shook his big head and charged again, both arms grabbing at Ben for a bear hug. Ben grabbed Renfro's right and spun into a rolling hip lock, flipping the big man to the ground in a hard fall.

Renfro got up slowly, his hair matted with dust and dirt, eyeing Ben warily. With a roar, he charged Ben for the third time, arms flailing wildly. He was big and strong, but he was no fighter. He had won all his previous brawls because none of his opponents were anything more than untrained street thugs themselves. This was the first time he had ever been hurt and it began to dawn on him that this smaller man was giving him the whipping that was promised. With no plan other than to grab and crush his tormentor, he closed the gap.

Ben watched the big man come and calmly set himself. He stepped inside the flailing arms and

EMPIRE

threw a devastating right uppercut with all his weight
behind it, straight to the point of Renfro's chin.

The watching riders swore later that Renfro went
all the way up on his toes and then clear off the
ground from the force of the savage blow. Ben
stepped out of the way as the momentum of the
charge propelled a now unconscious Renfro into the
fire, scattering coals and coffee everywhere as he
plowed the ground. Bear rode up and quickly
dabbed a loop over his boots, pulling him out of the
smoke and flames.

One of the riders shook his head in disgust.
'Damn! I was plannin' on havin' me a cup o' that
there coffee!'

'Who sent you?' Ben watched as the big man came
back to his senses.

Renfro rubbed his jaw and looked ruefully at Ben.
'I don't know who he is. Feller runs the Emporium
at Cook's Crossin' is also the postmaster and he said
he had a letter addressed to me. I was plumb surprised 'cause it was the first letter I ever got. It said
he knew I was a miner and if I was to watch your
diggin's and leave a report in the outhouse behind
the Trail's End, he'd pay me thirty a month and
found through the mail. That was six months ago,
and he paid each time.'

'What did he want to know about the mine?'

'Just what I estimated you were takin' out a month
in ore. I figgered he was plannin' to hold up a shipment, but he never asked about when you was

91

plannin' to move a load. Kinda puzzled me, but I didn't ask questions. It was a right easy job.' He glanced around at the hard faces.

'Until now I reckon.'

'I hear there's a gold strike over California way,' Ben said, 'and I hear the climate over there is somewhat healthier than around here.'

Renfro smiled through broken lips. 'You mean you're gonna turn me loose? After what I done?'

'As long as you're off my land by sunset. It's almost noon so you'd better hurry. And I don't advise ever coming back this way. I might take it wrong.'


'Rider comin'.'

Ben put down his pen and pushed back from the big roll-top desk. He walked to the door and stepped out on the porch where Bear was lounging. 'Who is it?'

'Can't tell. He don't set a horse like nobody I know.'

The rider slowly made his way up the trail and into the barnyard, obviously noting the placement of anyone who might pose a danger, a caution that made Ben smile. 'Light and set. There's coffee on if you're of a mind to.'

'You Ben Tower?' The rider was a tall, older man with a shock of gray hair and a quiet air of authority about him. He pulled back his coat and displayed a badge on his vest. 'I'm Harvey Davis, United States

Marshal for the territory and I've papers to serve on you.'

'That coffee's hot and fresh.'

Davis glanced sharply at Ben, a slow smile spreading across his face. 'You don't rile none too easy, do you? All right, I reckon I will have me a cup of that coffee you're trying so hard to sell.'

Ben studied the papers over his cup, and glanced at Marshal Davis. 'Who's disputing my claim to the Rafter T?'

'Don't rightly know. Judge Lowry just told me to serve these on you. You're to appear in his court next month at the territorial capital to defend your claim to this here valley.'

'What about this Judge Lowry? What sort of man is he?'

The marshal glanced over at Bear and back to Ben. Ben nodded at Bear who shrugged and stepped outside.

'I said I don't know who brought this action and I don't because the name ain't on the papers and I wasn't told. But I have my suspicions and if I'm right, you got serious troubles, son, because this man and Judge Lowry are thick as thieves and twice as crooked. Fact is, there ain't a lawyer at the capital that I would trust not to be either in cahoots or scared of this here feller and Lowry. Fact also is, this here Lowry is only a judge through a political appointment. All he knows about the law is what he's picked up from the shyster lawyers who use his court to steal.

'If I was you, I'd get me a lawyer from St Louis or maybe Santa Fe. If it helps any, I'll be sitting in on the hearing just to make sure Lowry stays fairly close to the up and up.'

Ben watched the marshal mount up and ride off. A door slammed in the bunkhouse and laughter came from the corral as another rider tried his hand at staying with Rowdy and lost. No one had ever ridden the old gelding, but Ben kept him anyway for reasons he couldn't put his finger on. Maybe they were cut from the same cloth.

Ben walked back into the house and found Mattie in the kitchen. 'I need to ride east to the telegraph and send a wire. I'll be back as soon as I can.'

Mattie nodded, kissed her husband and went back to kneading the day's bread.

# 8

Judge Lowry's courthouse was already packed when Ben strode across the dusty street and up the stairs to the boardwalk. The hotel clerk had informed Ben that the whole town knew about the Rafter T dispute and Ben was astonished to learn that his own name was also well known.

'Yes, sir, the whole territory knows about the Rafter T and Ben Tower! Why you're just about the biggest man in the territory, what with your timber business, the mine and your cattle ranchin' too!'

The clerk had showed him to his room, along with Bear and Clay Johnson, and by the time they reached the door, the clerk had told them more than a newspaper.

'Nobody knows who's layin' claim to the T, but it's rumored he has an air-tight case.' The clerk sadly shook his head. 'Folks say it's a shame, what with you helpin' other folks out and such, but the law is the law, I suppose.'

Ben stood in front of the courthouse doors for a moment and surveyed the street. Bear was lounging on the bench in front of the Emporium with his Sharps .50 close at hand and although Clay Johnson was nowhere to be seen, he knew the curly-headed gunman had taken up a vantage point somewhere nearby. Ben expected no shooting trouble, but with an obvious steal in the making, it made sense to be cautious.

The early morning sun felt good on his shoulders as he turned and pushed his way through the doors. The roar of excited voices died away as he heard his name whispered up and down the room, and curious faces turned to see him. Harvey Davis, the US Marshal, was seated at a table down front. He rose, turned, and nodded at Ben, waving him to a chair at the table. Ben seated himself and spoke quietly to Davis, 'Any word on who's shindig this is?'

'We'll know in a minute. Here comes Judge Lowry now.'

'All rise.'

The judge was a small, pompous-looking man who glanced coldly around the courtroom before seating himself. He pointedly ignored Ben and the marshal.

The clerk called out in a clear voice, 'The Territorial Court is now in session, Judge Thomas Lowry presiding. You may be seated.'

The judge waited for quiet and studied some

papers for a moment. He looked up and nodded at the clerk.

'In the case of legal ownership of the Rafter T,' the clerk intoned, 'Will the plaintiff come forward and present his case.'

'I'm here, your Honor.'

Ben turned and looked into the triumphant eyes of big Dan Goodwin . . . the same Dan Goodwin who had once tried to steal Bear's lost mesa herd from Ben.

So that was it! The failed attempt on his life at the ranch and again here in the territorial capital, and yet again on the trail home when the killers died in the flash flood. Then the surveillance of his mine by big Cab Renfro! Now it all made sense. Goodwin tried to take the property by having him killed, and, failing that, to steal it now with the help of a crooked judge.

It was a combination of vengeance and greed.

He glanced at Marshal Davis, who gave a slight nod, acknowledging that Dan Goodwin was indeed the man he had in mind when he spoke to Ben at the ranch.

Ben watched the judge's eyes make subtle contact with those of Goodwin and the obvious recognition of mutual intent. He wondered what the judge was to get out of this and the basis for Goodwin's claim to the land. He didn't have to wait long.

'Your honor, if it please the court, we would like to introduce the following evidence establishing Dan

Goodwin's legal right to the lands, buildings, cattle, timber, mines, and all other properties known as the Rafter T.'

'Come forward.'

'That's Jonathon Sneed, one of the crooked lawyers working with Judge Lowry,' Davis whispered. 'Whatever claims he has are almost certainly cooked and fraudulent but unless you have better, the judge will rule for Goodwin. The steal is on.'

The judge read the papers and glanced up at Goodwin. 'This here is a Spanish land grant made out to a Senor Louis Rodriguez for all the lands in that area including that known as the Rafter T. Do you have papers signing this grant over to you?'

'Indeed we do, your honor. Señor Rodriguez made a deed signing all the lands in the grant over to Mr Goodwin for the sum of five thousand dollars in gold. We also have the receipt.' The lawyer handed the papers to the judge who seemed to study them carefully.

'Where is Mister Rodriguez now?'

'Sadly, your honor, Mister Rodriguez moved back to Mexico where he passed away some years ago.'

Dan Goodwin had first learned of the Rodriguez land grant from idle campfire talk while planning to rob a wagon train. Intrigued, he questioned the narrator, Little Dave Mathers, and learned that Mathers had once worked for Rodriguez and knew where the grant was hidden. Little Dave also remarked on Rodriguez's well-known homesickness for old

Mexico. Goodwin immediately saw the possibilities and canceled plans to rob the wagon train. Two days later, Goodwin, Dooley Clowers, and Little Dave had the land grant and a tortured Señor Louis Rodriguez had signed papers deeding over the land to Goodwin and a receipt for money never paid, before he was killed and buried in a remote corner of the ranch. Goodwin also killed Little Dave Mathers and buried him on top of Rodriguez for good measure. No sense in having another witness and he never liked Little Dave anyway.

The locals were satisfied with the tale that Rodriguez had returned to Mexico because he had often told them he would someday. No one questioned the supposed sale of the ranch and Goodwin's take over. When Goodwin had his run-in with Ben Tower and learned of the Rafter T, he took the land grant to a forger in Santa Fe, who altered it to include the entire valley. To ensure that the forgery was never discovered, Goodwin simply killed the forger and made it look like a robbery.

'Yes, yes, I see. Very well, these papers look in order.' Judge Lowry rustled the papers importantly and looked over his glasses at the courtroom, noting the many nods in the audience, with satisfaction.

Davis leaned close to Ben. 'Sneed and Lowry had dinner together last night at the Emporium and Sneed handed the judge some papers to look over. Would you like to wager what those papers were?'

Dan Goodwin glanced over at Ben, caught his eye and smugly winked at him. To his surprise, Ben merely smiled. Goodwin looked immediately away, alarmed and searching his mind, trying to remember if they had made an error or possibly forgotten something. Satisfied that it was airtight, he relaxed, but a small kernel of doubt gnawed at him.

Judge Lowry cleared his throat and rapped with his gavel. The murmur in the courtroom died away and the crowd waited expectantly.

'In view of the overwhelming evidence presented by the plaintiff and counsel, the court finds that it must rule in favor of . . .'

'Hold on just a minute there, Judge.' A tall, well-dressed man with mutton-chop sideburns seated in the third row came to his feet. 'If it please the court, I have evidence to present in support of Mister Ben Tower's rightful claim to the property known as the Rafter T.'

Judge Lowry glanced nervously at Jonathon Sneed, who shrugged his shoulders and turned to Dan Goodwin for an answer. But Goodwin was staring blankly at the stranger, having no idea who he was or what evidence he might have.

Judge Lowry sighed and addressed the stranger. 'Just who might you be and what do you know of this case, sir?'

'I'm Chester T. Franklin, president and general manager of the St Louis and Southwestern Railroad, otherwise known as the SL & S.'

100

An astonished and excited courtroom erupted in chatter. The SL & S, once scheduled to take a southern route through Cook's Crossing, had been re-routed just last year through the territorial capital and was now only a few miles away. And here was the president of the SL & S himself! What could he possibly have to do with this case?

Sneed jumped to his feet. 'I object, your honor. The railroad has nothing to do with the matter at hand!'

'On the contrary, sir, the railroad has a great deal to do with this trial,' retorted Franklin, 'and I demand to be heard!'

A red-faced Judge Lowry rapped the gavel for silence. He looked cautiously from the railroad president to Sneed who nodded slightly. 'Well, sir, I'm going to rule that your testimony is irrelevant and that any business you may have with this court can wait until . . .'

Marshal Harvey Davis came abruptly to his feet, the chair he was sitting in falling backward and clattering on the courtroom floor. His voice boomed, 'Judge Lowry, as the US Marshal for this territory, I am authorized to investigate all crimes, including fraud and malfeasance in office, sir, even if it means hanging those responsible.'

A stunned Lowry stared at Davis. His eyes darted around the room, looking for assistance, but in vain. In a quavering voice, he asked, 'What are you referring to, Harvey? Why are you telling me this?'

The marshal smiled at the judge. 'Why, just in case it becomes necessary, Tom.'

The courtroom erupted in laughter. The reputation of the judge and the local lawyers was well known and Marshal Davis' sly warning was instantly understood by all present.

Thoroughly flustered, the judge rapped for order again and glanced from the smiling marshal to a furious Jonathon Sneed and decided to take his chances with whatever the railroad president had to say. After all, he might not have anything important to add anyway.

'All right, Mr Franklin, you may come forward.'

Dan Goodwin and lawyer Jonathon Sneed were glowering at Judge Lowry as the railroad president took a seat in the witness chair. Judge Lowry administered the oath for the first time that day, an oversight that did not escape the attention of anyone present. Judge Lowry leaned to his left and asked, 'Now, sir, what evidence have you that could possibly affect this case, sir?' He stole a glance at Sneed who ignored him.

Franklin's measured voice was strong and assured, 'Well, your honor, as you and all others well know, the SL & S is constructing a line that will soon pass through this fair city. And, as you also know, that line was originally to be routed south through the Cook's Crossing area and points west.'

'Yes, yes, we are all aware of that, but what about it?'

'Mister Ben Tower here came to my office over a year ago and made an excellent proposal that fared well for all involved. Since the original route was to pass through the southern tip of the Rafter T, his land was technically owned by the SL & S because the federal government granted us a twenty mile right of way on either side of the scheduled route, taking in the Rafter T and a good deal more.'

'Since Mister Tower is familiar with this territory from his days of exploration, he successfully demonstrated to us that the northern route was a far better option, both for commerce and for ease of construction. He further proposed that the SL & S trade him title to the lands we no longer needed in the south, in exchange for ties and bridge timbers that he would cut, mill, and deliver. The SL & S readily agreed and gave him deeds to the property.'

He paused and allowed the information to sink in. 'Furthermore, even if Mister Goodwin's land grant is genuine, it was never recorded and in any case, has been superseded by the United States government's power of eminent domain. Obviously, the railroad needs the ties and timbers Mister Tower has contracted to supply. Consequently, the SL & S has no intention of standing idly by and allowing the plaintiff to take land that is not his, and disrupt that supply.'

The courtroom sat in stunned silence. Judge Lowry stared at Chester T. Franklin as if he had grown a second head. The enormity of Franklin's words had sunk in on Dan Goodwin and his lawyer, Sneed, both of whom sat with their mouths agape, looking first to Franklin and then to Ben Tower.

Ben Tower came quietly to his feet. 'Your honor? I have a little evidence to present myself.' Judge Lowry waved his hand wearily at him and Ben approached the bench. Goodwin and Sneed looked at each other in alarm. Not only had they failed, this was quickly getting out of hand.

Ben reached into his coat pocket and pulled out an envelope filled with papers and handed it to the judge. 'These are deeds to my properties, your honor, all properly filed and recorded many months ago.'

Judge Lowry's eyes widened as he read the papers and his jaw dropped. He looked at Goodwin and Sneed in horror and back at Ben. 'Is this right?'

Ben nodded. 'That's right, Judge. My deal with the SL & S was for the entire southern right of way grant. I own not only the Rafter T, but all the lands included in the railroad's original right of way, including the town of Cook's Crossing.'

Ben turned and looked Dan Goodwin square in the face. 'That includes the land Dan Goodwin calls his ranch.'

## 9

Chester Franklin leaned back in his chair and lit a cigar. 'I hear Marshal Davis decided to make good on his threat and look into that Spanish land grant business. He figures it's a fake and aims to prove it. Lowry and Sneed are both in a panic and Dan Goodwin left town right after the trial. You figure to boot him off your land and claim the ranch, Ben?'

Franklin and Ben, along with Bear and Clay Johnson, were enjoying supper at the Emporium. Ben signaled to the waitress for more coffee.

'Well, when I first learned that he was ranching on land that was rightfully mine, I decided to meet with him and make some sort of arrangement that would be profitable to both of us and let our past difficulty be forgotten. But when I discovered today that he was the one who put a price on my head and nearly got me killed, I lost all interest in mending any fences with Dan Goodwin. I've been informed that he intends to make a drive east to sell all his cattle

105

and pocket the proceeds. Since he's not putting up a fight, I suspect that he did not come across the Rodriguez ranch legally and doesn't want to be around when Marshall Davis starts digging into it. He intends to pack up everything of value and torch the house and barn.'

'You gonna let him get away with that, boss?' Clay put down his fork. 'Say the word and I'll take some of the boys over there and put a stop to it.'

Ben smiled. 'From what I've heard, fire is the best way to get rid of bedbugs and cockroaches. No, I'm told the buildings weren't much account in the first place, so maybe Goodwin is doing me a favor by getting rid of them for me. Besides, we have our own drive to make, and I'll need all hands.'

Bear sipped his coffee and glanced at Ben. 'Boss, I heard that Dooley Clowers was in town for the trial, but no one saw him leave with Goodwin. He ain't never forgot how you threw him in that icehouse back in Cook's Crossin'.'

Ben shrugged. 'If he's hunting me, there's nothing I can do to stop him.'

'Just warnin' you. He's a bad one. Some say he's killed three men.'

'Which way were they looking at the time?'

'Well sure, but a bullet in the back will kill you just as dead as one you're lookin' at.'

Bear and Clay left for the hotel while Ben and Chester Franklin had after-dinner cigars and brandy. They listened idly to the still-excited talk of the trial and were aware of many glances in their direction. Sneed and Judge Lowry had seemed invincible to the locals, so watching a rancher like Ben Tower utterly destroy both of them, shaped up to be an historical event.

Finally, Franklin excused himself and left. Ben listened a few more minutes and then paid his bill and stepped outside. He paused for a moment on the boardwalk, finishing his cigar, enjoying the cool night air. Outside town, a coyote called, and a local dog yapped his answer. The moon was dark, and the only light came from the Emporium windows and the Cattleman's Saloon across the street and nearly a block away. Somewhere a protesting pump squeaked as someone drew water for the evening. The night was cloudless, and the stars were brilliant in the ebony sky.

Across the street, a loafer rose from a bench, stretched and ambled slowly down the stairs to step into the dust of the street.

Ben flicked the ash from his cigar, took a last puff and ground it out under his heel. He had just turned to go when the shadowy figure stopped in the middle of the street, and the light from the Emporium window revealed his face. It was Dooley Clowers.

'Too bad, Tower. I planned to shoot you in the back as you walked by. You would have never felt a thing, but you stayed up on that boardwalk too long. Now you'll see it comin'.' Ben could see Clowers' yellow-toothed grin in the lamplight. 'I owe you one, Tower, and this time your luck has run out. We got you boxed up like a rat.'

'This one's out of it, boss,' Clay called out from across the street in the shadows. 'He ain't interested in testin' this scattergun.'

'And if that jasper hidin' in the alley wants to see tomorrow, he'd best stay out of this one too.' Bear's voice came from a second-story window where Ben could see a rifle barrel, and out of the corner of his eye, he saw a man stand in the shadows and slowly raise his hands.

Clowers licked his lips and a look of uncertainty moved across his face. He shifted his feet and wiped his right hand on his greasy shirt.

'Looks like you lost your help, Dooley. You don't have to do this, you know. You can turn around and head for Texas and live until somebody else kills you.'

Clowers' eyes narrowed and his face tightened in decision. 'To hell with that!'

His arm dropped, and Ben's gun was bucking in his hand, firing three shots in an almost steady roar. Clowers sank to his knees, a puzzled look on his face. He tried to raise his arm to fire his own shots, but the gun somehow slipped out of his fingers, suddenly far too heavy for his weak grip. He stared at it, bewildered, and sagged slowly to the ground. Then Ben Tower was standing over him and Dooley's mouth worked but the words never came. He was dead.

The street filled with onlookers from the Emporium and the Cattleman's Saloon, staring at the body of Dooley Clowers and discussing the day's events in hushed voices. Bear and Clay quickly found Ben and related their accounts of the shooting to Marshal Davis who nodded and placed their prisoners under arrest.

Davis looked at Ben ruefully. 'When will you folks be leaving? Trouble seems to follow you and I like a peaceable town.'

'We'll be riding out in the morning. I've a ranch to run.'

Clay Johnson studied Ben thoughtfully. 'Ranch? Sounds more like an empire to me, boss!'

# 10

'What about the folks at Cook's Crossing?'

Mattie placed a plate of bacon and eggs in front of Ben, along with thick slabs of fresh, homemade bread, slathered in butter. Ben silently gave thanks once again for having the good sense to listen to Mattie about raising chickens, pigs, and keeping the dairy cattle from the lost wagon train.

'What will you do about them, Ben? Lots of them are good honest folks who thought the land would be theirs.'

'And so it will be, Mattie. I've hired a surveyor to map out the town and assign lots according to the way the town folks have it laid out. When he's done, I'll make out deeds to most folks, but I'll keep all the land in the streets and lots not claimed.'

'What did you mean by "most folks"?'

'There are one or two who don't shape up to be folks who'll do their fair share. I'll give them a chance, but if they don't change their ways, I'll keep

110

that land and move them on down the river.'

'Don't become a man judging others, Ben,' Mattie said quietly, 'and don't let all this wealth and power go to your head. You have the right by ownership to decide who you will favor and who you will not, but as a man, you have an obligation to let other folks have their faults, just as we all have our faults.'

Ben started to retort and then caught himself. He looked over his coffee mug at Mattie's gentle eyes and he knew she was right. 'You win, Mattie. I'll deed over everyone's lots and let them sort it out. And you're right ... I do have my faults, although picking an intelligent, lovely, and good woman to be my wife was not one of them.'

Mattie rose and patted his hand, a faint blush highlighting her cheeks. She loved and admired Ben more with each passing year and it pleased her greatly to know he valued her advice. She started to leave the room and then suddenly stopped and turned to Ben as if she had just remembered something. 'By the way, while you're counting your blessings, you can add one more. There's another child on the way.'

She turned and walked down the hall, adding over her shoulder, 'At least I hope it's just one this time!'

# 11

'Oh, this is so exciting, Ben!' A smiling and radiant Mattie pushed the carriage containing little Henry and one-month-old daughter, Julie, both sound asleep. The twins, Joseph and Jeremiah, and their younger brother Walt, now three, walked with their father down the Denver boardwalk.

The territory was now the new State of Colorado, it was 1876, and a major celebration was underway in Denver, the new state capitol. Later in the day, Ben and Mattie were invited podium guests of Governor John Routt, last Territorial Governor and first State Governor. But now, the parade was about to start, so Ben was looking for a good place to watch the proceedings. He pointed across the street and up.

'The Emporium balcony has some room, Mattie. Let's head over there.'

Wide-eyed and fascinated, the older boys lined the Emporium railing and watched the parade. The buildings on both sides of the street were draped in red, white, blue bunting, as were the lampposts and hitching rails. Below, wagons, horses, and riders, decked out in their finest, paraded noisily by, as firecrackers thrown by young boys crackled everywhere amid great whoops of laughter. Ben grinned and looked at Mattie who smiled and shook her head.

For nearly an hour, the parade went on until the rear was brought up by a finely-mounted group of United States Cavalry. As Ben had seen them do a couple of blocks away, when in front of the building and on command, the line wheeled right and presented arms. They then fired a volley of blanks and wheeled left to continue down the street. Ben applauded with the rest of the crowd and then helped Mattie gather up the children.

On the boardwalk again, Ben nodded and smiled as people recognized him and he shook hand after hand. The story of how he had outsmarted Judge Lowry and lawyer Sneed was now legend and had grown until only a small portion of it was actually true.

Marshal Davis' investigation revealed that Goodwin, Sneed, and Lowry had pulled off several similar but much smaller land and cattle thefts and that both Sneed and Lowry had received payoffs from Goodwin. Davis had also discovered the grave of Senor Rodriguez after questioning a Mexican who had a silver belt suspiciously like the one Rodriguez had owned. The Mexican admitted to witnessing the burial of Rodriguez and the subsequent murder and burial of Little Dave Mathers. He returned later and robbed the grave, getting the silver belt and many other items, including Little Dave's gun and belt.

Sneed and Lowry were both behind bars and Marshal Davis had a warrant for Dan Goodwin for the murders of Senor Rodriguez and Little Dave Mathers, but Goodwin had disappeared some years ago. It was rumored that he had been robbed and killed in Kansas after selling his cattle, but there was no official record of such a killing.

Ben's holdings were so vast that there were plans underway to take him to court in an effort to redistribute the land. The argument was being circulated that no man should have so much land and wealth, and Ben could see where a court might be sympathetic to that plea. Of course, those who wanted and felt entitled to his land, had done nothing to earn it. While he was damming up waterholes, building corrals, and feeding steers trapped in blizzards, they were warm, safe, and comfortable in cities far to the east.

To stave off such attacks, he was already mapping out large sections to be designated as State Parks, open to the public free of charge, but still in his possession and with the provision that he retain all grazing and mineral rights. He hoped that might influence the court should a suit be brought. He also had the influence of many men of power, including the new Governor, if needed, but it had been some of them who had warned him of plans to challenge his holdings.

He had already moved much of the property into a family holding, further spreading out ownership. He had also given the O'Hara family two-thousand acres of good farmland. Then he deeded Clay Johnson and Medicine Hawk a thousand acres each and helped all of them set up houses and barns. Bear was made the same offer, but he declined, preferring to stay on at the Rafter T.

Ben was also in the process of setting up farms on the tillable portion of the land, to be leased out on shares to farmers. If they proved out, he was going to make deals allowing them to own their farms in due time. It was both good business and an argument of good stewardship should it come to a court case.

This was the first trip to a city for the older boys and they were fascinated with all the great buildings and noise. They pointed out each new thing to their father who patiently explained its purpose. At last they reached their destination and stepped off the boardwalk and on to the lush grass of the city park.

'Where's Bear?' asked Mattie. Bear had driven Mattie's carriage with the children while Ben rode alongside. 'He's around somewhere,' Ben replied. 'Probably having a beer at the Cattleman's and telling a few lies.'

The new stage and podium were set up next to the old bandstand and as they neared the park facilities, they could hear the town orchestra tuning up. A smiling official spotted them and led them to a table beneath a large oak. While the three older boys began to play with others their age, Mattie draped a vanity blanket over her shoulder and began to nurse Julie. In a couple of hours, it would be time to nurse Henry who was not yet weaned. She shot an accusing look at Ben who developed a sudden interest in his boots.

After a picnic lunch, the crowd gathered around the podium and the official sought out Ben and Mattie to seat them on the platform. Mattie declined, not wanting to leave her children with strangers, so Ben mounted the steps alone and took his seat. One after another, speakers rose and said their piece until it was Governor Routt's turn. He spoke to the wonders of Statehood and of the many pioneering men who were responsible for the success. One by one he introduced them to the crowd who applauded enthusiastically.

When it came Ben's turn, the crowd came to its feet and roared its approval, much to the delight of the grinning Governor. Ben stood and waved his hat and the crowd roared even louder. As Ben's eyes swept the mass of faces, he suddenly glimpsed a vaguely familiar, unsmiling face, but when he tried to find the face again, it had disappeared. Try as he might, he could not put a name to it. He shrugged and continued smiling and waving at the crowd.

The applause eventually died down and he regained his seat. The governor droned on and he glanced over at the table where Mattie was sitting.

She was gone, probably rounding up the boys.

Finally, the speech was over but as Ben stood to leave, the Governor pulled him aside, a thoughtful look on his face. 'You've made a real name for yourself, young man, and it looks like you have quite a following. We'll be needing representation in Washington soon, and I may call upon you to run for office.' At Ben's startled look, the Governor smiled and said, 'No need to say anything today, just think it over and let me know if you have an interest.'

They were leaving the reviewing stand when Ben felt a hand on his sleeve. It was Bear, and his face was drawn. 'You'd best come quick. It's Mattie!'

Suddenly Ben remembered the face in the crowd. It was older, the beard and hair were gray, and there was a madness in the eyes, but there was no doubt about it.

It was Dan Goodwin.

# 12

'She's lost a lot of blood and there's some damage to her right kidney, but I was able to get to the bullet and stop the bleeding.'

The doctor handed Ben the short, fat piece of lead in a tin basin with Mattie's blood still on it.

'Probably some drunk cowhand celebrating and not thinking.' The doctor shook his head and wiped his spectacles. 'Bound to happen sooner or later. We have a law about discharging firearms inside the city limits, but the town marshal doesn't enforce it because he does it too after a few drinks!'

Mattie's face was ashen, and her forehead was almost cold to the touch. She was conscious, but said nothing, and her eyes were closed. When Ben had asked if she knew what had happened to her, she gave a slight nod, tried to speak, but failed. Guessing her intent, Ben assured her that the children were in excellent hands and he had located a wet nurse for Julie. She nodded again, and a fleeting smile crossed her lips. She closed her eyes again.

'She needs absolute rest and she needs to take nourishment in order to replace the blood she lost. I think her kidney will heal satisfactorily if there's no infection. We should have a fair idea of how this will turn out within a week. In the meantime, I suggest you leave her here where she'll be cared for night and day.' The doctor glanced at Ben. 'From this point on, it's all in God's hands, son. I've done all I know how to do. I make no promises.'

Ben washed the blood off the bullet in his hotel room basin and examined it carefully. The doctor knew his medicine but not much about firearms. It didn't come from a pistol any cowboy would carry. It was a derringer bullet, probably a .41 rimfire caliber, and had been fired at close range. Such ammunition lost much of its power in just a few yards and probably would not have even penetrated Mattie's skin had it happened the way the doctor described.

It was also no accident. It was intended to punish Ben by taking away what was most dear to him in retaliation for what he had taken from the shooter . . . his ranch and his pride. Dan Goodwin was back, and the war was not over. It had just begun.

Ben gave Bear his instructions. 'I can't wait or the trail will grow cold, so I'm riding out in the morning. You stay here and keep an eye on Mattie and the children. I sent Clay back to the ranch to tend to the business.'

'You know he's plannin' an ambush.' Bear shook

his head in disgust. 'He'll be layin' for you, sure as anythin'. He made no effort at the livery stable to cover up who he is and where he's goin', so he expects you to follow him and he'll be waitin'.'

'Can't be helped. I'll have a better chance knowing he'll be gunning for me than have him come at me some other day when I don't expect it. I left word at the marshal's office, so when Harvey Davis gets back, he can follow and lend me a hand. You just watch over the family for me while I'm gone, Bear.' Ben looked hard at the old cowboy. 'And if I don't come back, you see to things as best you can. I'm obliged to you for that.'

Bear lifted his hat and scratched his head mournfully. 'Sure I will, but you just see to it that you *do* come back. If I'd wanted a bunch of kids to look after, I would have had some my own self.'

The next morning, Ben studied the tracks in the stall where Goodwin's horse had been stabled. The hostler said it was a big black and that he had also replaced two shoes while boarding the horse, so the tracks were fairly distinctive.

'Big feller with gray hair except some was still yeller here and there. Had him a full beard and was wearing a tan duster last I seen of him.' He pointed down the street. 'Rode off south, easy as you please, sort of humming to himself.' He glanced at Ben. 'Friend of yours?'

'No, just someone I'm looking for. You sure he went south?'

'Yup. I watched him ride out and maybe fifteen minutes later, I seen him crest that hill south of town. He stopped there and wheeled around, looking this way like he was checking his back trail or looking to be followed.' He shrugged and looked over at Ben. 'If you're going after him, you better know that he had a crazy look about him. I think he's a dangerous man, mister, and I also think he expects to be followed.'

The trail was one a blind man could follow, and it made Ben uneasy. Goodwin was weaving a trap for sure and Ben was deliberately riding right into it. But what choice did he have? If he didn't face him now, he'd have to face him later and who knew when that might be? It was better to hunt him down now and be done with it.

The problem was that by shooting Mattie, Goodwin had already proved that he was no longer sane, because a man who harmed a woman in the west was marked for death and would be hunted down and killed. When it became known that Mattie's injury was no accident and that Dan Goodwin was responsible, he would be a marked man and sooner or later would stretch a rope from some lonely tree. Goodwin knew that but shot Mattie anyway, so if Ben didn't stop him now, who would be next? One of the children? All of them?

For a moment, he almost regretted not turning the herd over to Goodwin, so long ago. Maybe then, none of this would have happened and Mattie would be safe at home. But just as quickly, he knew that before too long, he would have crossed Goodwin's path anyway and that this fight was the inevitable way of things. Fate will not be denied.

On every ridge he came to, he simply rode up and over, deliberately exposing himself, hoping to draw some over-eager fire, instead of waiting until he rode into point blank range. And on every ridge, the hair stood up on the back of his neck as he tensed and waited for the slam of a bullet.

He camped that night under a large oak with a granite wall protecting his back. He counted on a deep collection of dried oak leaves to warn him of approaching danger. He cleared an area of leaves and picketed his horse where it could graze on the exposed grass. He built no fire, eating a cold supper of canned beans and jerky. For a long time, he watched the valley to the south and listened. He heard nothing but the night sounds of the wild and was just about to turn in when he thought he caught a glimmer of light out of the corner of his eye. He turned and watched intently but saw nothing for a long time and was about to give up when he saw the flare-up of a far-off campfire as someone added fuel.

Was it Goodwin? If so, why was he so far off the trail? The fire was a good two miles east of where a traveler would be camped while following this route . . . unless he was backtracking in order to set up an ambush. Had Goodwin built a fire thinking it could not be seen so far off the trail? Had he made a mistake?

Ben was back in the saddle and without breakfast while the sun was still two full hours from rising. If an ambush was planned, he wanted to be there before Goodwin. He knew that from the location of the mysterious campfire, there was a dry stream bed which a man could easily follow back to the main trail and wait for someone following his tracks. Ben planned to be there first and set up his own ambush.

The sun was just breaking over the horizon and warm on his back as he took his position. Below was the stream bed, dry and rocky with a sand bar here and there where floods had deposited them. There was no sound except for a lone raven lookout occasionally cawing from its perch high atop a dead pine. He'd picketed his horse nearly a mile back, just in case it was tempted to whinny a greeting should a rider come up the dry waterway.

An hour later, he was about to give it up and head back when he heard a slowly-walking horse coming up the stream bed. He pushed forward slightly from his position under some sagebrush and watched the bend in the creek bed for the rider to appear. Sweat ran down his cheek as he steadied the rifle and eared back the hammer, covering it with his left hand to muffle the clicking sounds of metal on metal. The sound of rocks rattling under hoofs echoed along the walls, as the horse slowly picked its way among the water-rounded and treacherous stones. A mosquito buzzed around his ear and some-where, another raven called to the lookout.

Then, for a long time, the horse stopped. Had the rider heard him cocking the hammer? Or was he simply pausing to listen? Then, it came on again, a little faster this time and Ben tensed, his finger finding the trigger and the sights aligned on the spot where the horse must first appear as it came around the bend. Suddenly its head appeared, and it stopped, a big black, his head high and listening, nostrils wide as it checked the air for the smell of danger. Satisfied, it finally stepped out, and Ben could see it was riderless.

Puzzled, Ben pushed forward for a better look and a bullet slammed into the granite shelf where he had been lying, whining wickedly away in a nasty ric-ochet. Instantly he dove behind a boulder, but not before spotting a rifle barrel on the facing hill across the creek. So that was why the horse took so long! Its rider had gotten off somewhere to climb the hill for the ambush and had allowed his horse to simply wander! When Ben had moved forward, he had been spotted immediately, causing a hasty shot which had nearly been successful.

Ben stayed below the ridgeline and quickly moved to his right. He eased up behind an outcropping and peered through a crack between rocks. After a moment, he spotted the rifle barrel, eased his own rifle forward, and waited. He was rewarded when a shoulder appeared just to the right of the rifle. He sighted slightly above it and squeezed off a shot. He heard the hard whap of a bullet striking flesh and the rifle disappeared, followed by a violent thrashing in the bushes, accompanied by several groans. Then silence.

Ben waited for a long time, but nothing moved. Finally, he began working back to the trail, a quarter of a mile to his right, where he could cross the stream bed out of range and out of sight. From there, he could work his way behind Goodwin's last known position and determine his condition, dead or alive.

The trail dipped down to the stream bed between two outcroppings on the north bank and then exited into a grove of large cottonwood on the south. Ben studied the far bank for several minutes from the concealment of the rocks and listened, but heard no sound except the calling of ravens. Finally, he eased out and stepped onto the trail. Instantly, a rifle spoke from the cottonwoods across the waterway, slamming him in the midsection, and he felt himself falling.

'You're savvy, I'll give you that, but it won't help you now.' Ben looked up and into the eyes of a mad man. Goodwin's shirt was gone, used for bandages to bind up his bleeding left shoulder, his left arm dangling uselessly. But in his right, he held a big, Colt Paterson pistol, hammer eared back and pointed at Ben's forehead.

Ben weakly felt for his own pistol and Goodwin laughed. 'Hell, the first thing I did was take your guns!' He grinned. 'Wouldn't want nobody to get hurt, now would we?'

His smile faded. 'Now I never harmed no woman before and she sure looked surprised when I done it. The crowd was all yelling their fool heads off at you on that stage, so nobody even heard it.'

He cocked his head and peered down on Ben with oddly vacant eyes. 'Well, no sense in wasting time.' He bent low and leveled the pistol at Ben's forehead. 'Too bad she had to die to get your attention.'

'She's not dead.' Ben looked defiantly at Goodwin. 'But you will be, just as soon as the word gets out that you shot a woman.'

'Maybe so, but you won't be caring about that or anything else.'

Dan Goodwin's finger tightened on the trigger and Ben flinched at the roar of a gunshot. He saw Goodwin stagger backwards, a shocked look on his face, and fall flat on his back, the Paterson firing harmlessly into the air. Then Bear was standing over Ben, the smoke still curling slowly from his Sharps .50.

'Where're you hit?'

'I don't know. Help me up.'

After regaining his feet, Ben pulled up his shirt and found a large, rapidly spreading bruise on his abdomen and a badly bent belt buckle, but no blood and no open wound. He grinned at Bear and then his eyes narrowed.

'I thought I told you to watch over Mattie!'

Bear backed away, his hands and palms stretched out in front of him in feigned fear.

'Now, boss, that's just what I did. When I went to the doctor's to check on her yesterday mornin', she was sittin' up in bed eatin' breakfast, cool as you please. Doc said it was a miracle she was alive at all, much less hungry and orderin' folks around! Then she got around to askin' after you and when I told her what you were doin', she reared up and ordered me to go after you straight off, so here I am.

'I found your horse back up the trail a mite and then I heard the shots, so I come a-runnin' and when I saw you on the ground and Dan Goodwin fixin' to shoot you, I just naturally cut loose and let her fly.'

Bear paused and scratched his beard. 'Boss, I surely do respect your orders and all, but I'd far rather have you mad at me than Mattie, and that there's a fact.'

# 13

'Who is he and what's his business with us, Ben?'
Mattie poured her husband another cup of coffee,
and picked up his breakfast dishes.

Ben looked up from the letter. 'His name is
Farnsworth, Mattie, Reginald Farnsworth. He repre-
sents a group of English investors who have taken an
interest in American ranching. In fact, several large
western ranchers sold out completely to English
investors and then they stayed on as managers.'

Mattie sat down across the table. 'What does this
Farnsworth fellow have in mind for the Rafter T? I
wouldn't want to sell out, Ben, or even sell a con-
trolling interest. I love it here, and it's a fine place to
raise a family.'

'Nor would I. The twins are nine years old now,
and I want each of them to take some of their savings
and buy a hundred head of cattle from the Rafter T
later this spring. I want them to move them up on

mountain pastures for the summer. They need to learn the business, and there's no better way to learn than to manage real cows and real money, especially when it's their own money.'

Ben grinned at Mattie's skeptical look. 'They'll be fine, Mattie. Bear and Digger Jones will be right there to guide them along, and they won't even know they're learning something. They're good boys, and I'm proud of them.

'As far as Mister Farnsworth is concerned, I have no interest in selling or leasing any part of the Rafter T, but I am open to going shares on a cattle investment, or possibly on some new stamp mills for the mine. I might even want to invest in a new, steam-powered saw mill. There's enough timber on the abandoned railroad right of way to supply a large mill for the next fifty years.'

'When will this Mr Farnsworth get here, Ben?'

'His letter says he'll be here tomorrow.' Ben rose and grinned at his worried-looking wife. 'He's English, not royalty, Mattie. He's nothing but the British version of a banker. Just be your usual, charming self.'

Ben stepped outside, and Mattie went to her cupboard to check on her best dishes.

Joseph and Jeremiah, better known as Joe and Jerry to the hands, had spent the last two days mucking out the horse stables and barn where Mattie kept three milk cows. It was hard, dirty work, but their father expected them to carry their share of the load, and they did, with only the usual, good-natured grumbling he had come to expect from them.

The team waited patiently as the boys filled the manure spreader for the last time, before pulling it to Mattie's two-acre garden and spreading the contents for fertilizer. They then drove the team down into the creek bed and washed the spreader down with buckets of water and a scrubbing with a couple of old brooms. Their pa was a stickler for keeping his equipment clean and in good repair, and Lord help the man who failed to comply.

The boys put the spreader back in the shed and then inspected their work with their father. Ben carefully examined each stall and the dairy stanchions for cleanliness and fresh straw while the boys anxiously looked on. Finally, he nodded his head and pointed at the tool shed. 'Are your poles in good order?'

Ben had promised the boys a day off to go fishing as soon as the spring chores were done, and the bend in the river known as 'the hole' was reportedly teeming with large, native trout this year, so they were fairly itching to try their luck. Although they'd already secretly checked their poles a dozen times in the last few days, they ran to the tool shed to get them out and check them one more time.

Ben watched them run off, and felt a familiar swelling in his chest. His oldest sons, identical twins except for a small birthmark on Joe's back, were turning out to be good, steady, and willing hands, even at their age. His son Walter was also showing an interest in the ranch, but he was the scholarly one. He did his chores willingly and cheerfully, but every spare minute was spent with a book. Young Henry was solemn and thoughtful, his intelligent eyes missing nothing. He was fiercely defensive of the whole family, but especially his sister, Julie, one year his junior. At five years of age, Henry was already the fighter of the family, and his father had to keep a tight rein on him. A boy a year older and much larger than Henry had pulled Julie's hair at school, and Henry instantly had him on the ground, giving him a bloody nose.

To the west, clouds were building up over the peaks, as they had been doing each day for a week, but without delivering the promised rain. Last year was unusually dry, and this year was shaping up to be the same. So far, the water was adequate, but a rancher always worried about water.

In two weeks, spring roundup and branding would begin. The Rafter T had registered four brands and two other ranches would be sending reps to check on their own brands. It was a good time of year, and Ben looked forward to it. Winter months were often hard, with limited travel, so spring brought neighbors together again, and branding fires saw a lot of back-slapping, hand shaking, and friendly grins. It was a place where men could be men and enjoy each other's company.

Ben mounted up and rode slowly along the dusty wagon road to the western slope, and then followed an old game trail up to the tree line. Winding around through the cool cathedrals of tall pines, he found his way to a favorite rocky outcropping where he could see the entire ranch from horseback. The valley was cloaked in the lush green of early spring, and the dark backs of grazing cattle dotted the land.

Along the eastern slope, he could just make out the top of the stamp mill, and the white streak of the slag pile. He had quietly made plans to move the stamp mill to the south another few miles, because the constant dull sound of the hammers reached all the way to the ranch-house. Mattie had said nothing, but he knew the noise disturbed her. She liked the sounds of a working ranch, but not the steady throb of the mill. It would mean hauling the ore a few miles, but Ben knew it would be appreciated, and he, too, liked a quiet evening on the front porch.

The many stacks of hay put up for last winter were now down to the ground, and again, he looked hopefully to the skies. A few good summer rains meant one and possibly two additional hay cuttings, and he'd need every bit of it come winter. Otherwise, he'd have to buy hay, and that would eat into the profits on his cattle. He mounted up and headed back down to the ranch-house.

Ben was in the tack room the following morning when he heard a wagon and several horses pull into the barnyard. Clay Johnson poked his head in the door. 'Visitors, boss. Some English dude and his son.' Clay grinned, and lowered his voice. 'You ought to see that kid's get-up!'

Reginald Farnsworth was a tall, thin man, with an aristocratic bearing, and his son was about the same age as the twins. But any resemblance stopped there. The twins wore range clothes on the ranch, while this young man looked like he was about to take in an opera in Denver. He wore knee-high blue pants with a matching frock coat, frilled shirt, and a blue cap with a ribbon to top it all off. Ben looked back to Farnsworth and nodded.

'I reckon you'd be Mister Farnsworth. I'm Ben Tower, and this is the Rafter T.'

Reginald Farnsworth dismounted and took Ben's offered hand, with a surprisingly firm grip. 'How do you do, sir? I am indeed a Farnsworth as is my son, Jack, here.' He looked over at his son, and then back at Ben.

'You may be wondering why he is dressed so inappropriately. You see, my wife is traveling with us, but declined to visit a ranch. She stayed at our hotel in Denver, but insisted that Jack wear what she believes to be proper attire for calling on strangers.' He stopped and pursed his lips. 'My wife is rather, shall we say, set in her ways. Thus, poor Jack, who wanted to wear range clothing, is instead fit to attend a tea party.'

Ben grinned and walked over to Jack, still mounted on his horse. 'I have twin boys just about your size. Would you like to meet them and change

133

clothes? They have plenty, and they won't mind at all.'

'That would be most kind of you, sir. I am rather uncomfortable.'

Ben heard Clay mutter something and looked at him. Clay silently pointed over Ben's shoulder and Ben turned around in time to see Joseph and Jeremiah standing in the barn door staring at Jack Farnsworth. They slowly turned to look at one another and broke out in loud laughter. They pounded each other on the back and laughed some more, finally collapsing on the ground and holding their sides.

Jack Farnsworth slid off his horse and walked over to the twins, waiting. When they looked up at him, he asked, 'Don't you have a mother?'

'What? What are you talking about? Of course we have a mother!'

They scrambled to their feet and stared at him. He looked like a sissy, but he was not afraid.

'Doesn't your Mum dress you up sometimes when you don't want to?'

The twins shrugged. 'Maybe, but not like that! You talk funny too . . . like a sissy boy!'

'I can whip either one of you anytime.'

Joseph's mouth dropped open.

'You? Why, you couldn't whip my little sister!'

'I can whip both of you, one at a time. I wouldn't judge a book by its cover.'

'What does that mean?'

'It means don't decide who I am by how I'm dressed.'

Reginald Farnsworth moved next to Ben. 'Ben? May I call you Ben? And would you kindly call me Reggie?'

Ben nodded.

'Ben, Jack can probably do what he says. They're all about the same size, true, but Jack has had some training and he's quite good at fisticuffs. I'd better stop him.'

Ben shook his head and smiled. 'No, I think this might be a good lesson for the boys. Let's let them sort it out if you're willing, Reggie.' Ben found himself liking the Englishman.

'Very well. It shouldn't take long, and I quite agree. Let boys be boys.'

Jeremiah pushed ahead of his brother and threw his hat into the dust. He doubled his fist and threw an overhand haymaker at Jack. Jack stepped sideways and let the blow slip over his left shoulder while delivering three fast jabs with his left to the nose and face of Jeremiah, who then promptly joined his hat in the dirt.

Jeremiah got to his feet, and his hand went to his nose, coming away red with blood. For a moment, he stared at Jack, open-mouthed.

'Say, how do you do that? I never even saw it coming! Can you teach us that?'

'I will if you'll loan me some decent range clothes.'

All three boys ran to the house, whooping and yelling.

Reginald glanced at Ben. 'I said it wouldn't take long, but that was even faster than I thought!'

Ben grinned. 'The boys are going fishing today. Looks like I'd better rig another pole.'

Business was discussed over coffee, and Ben was pleased to learn that Reggie's clients wanted to invest in cattle, and possibly mining. They had no interest in buying ranches. They settled a deal on cattle, and Ben suggested a ride to the mine.

Ben watched as Reggie examined a piece of ore he had pulled off the cart. To his surprise, Reggie dug a jeweler's glass out of his vest and peered closely at the specimen, turning it over and over. He obviously knew what he was doing. Ben's respect for the man grew once again. Finally, Reggie turned to Ben with an excited grin on his face.

'I say! This is incredibly rich ore, Ben! I'd have to have a few random samples assayed, of course, but I'll want to recommend this to my investors. They'll back you on men and equipment.'

Ben and Reggie were sitting on the porch, enjoying coffee and cigars when Bear pounded down the road and into the barnyard, his horse lathered and winded. Alarmed, Ben rose and walked to the railing. Bear was wide-eyed and breathless.

'The boys are gone, Ben! I went to check on them and they're gone. Someone stacked some rocks and left this note under the top one.'

The note was brief and to the point. If Ben wanted the boys back, he was to drive alone down the road toward Cook's Crossing, and bring ten thousand in cash. The note said the ranch was being watched and anything that looked suspicious would result in the boys' deaths.

'Get the buckboard harnessed, Bear, and tell Clay Johnson to come to the house.' Ben turned to Reggie. 'I know your son is in this too, but it says I'm to come alone, so I'll have to ask you to stay here.' He looked the other man in the eye. 'I plan to find out where our boys are, and when I know, we'll both go, Reggie.'

Ben instructed Clay Johnson who left immediately. Mattie walked into the room and Ben gave her the news. He explained what he had in mind, and she nodded. Her eyes moistened, but she blinked back her tears.

'Who would do this, Ben?'

Ben looked at her thoughtfully.

'I hadn't considered that, Mattie. Someone who knows us, I suppose. Someone who thinks we have cash money. Maybe I'll know him when I see him.'

Ben found his leather valise, and gave it to Bear with instructions. He checked the loads in both his Winchester and his belt gun, placing the Winchester in the boot of the buckboard. He glanced one more time at his pocket-watch, and looked off to the south where the boys should have been. He had delayed long enough for his instructions to be underway. He embraced Mattie one more time, and climbed onto the seat. Taking up the reins, he drove slowly out of the yard.

The road to Cook's Crossing ran mostly on the flat grassland, but at one point, it ran up the slope and through the timber to avoid a marshy area on the lowland. It was here that Ben expected the kidnapper to appear and he was not disappointed. An unkempt, long-haired man stepped out from behind a large pine and held up his hand. He was armed with a double-barreled shotgun, and Ben did not recognize him, although there was something a little familiar about him.

'Hold up there! You Ben Tower?' The man peered closely at Ben, obviously unsure.

Ben didn't know him and he apparently didn't know Ben either. Ben stared at him a moment and then slowly nodded his head.

'That's right. I'm Ben Tower. You the man who took my boys?'

'You bring the money? Don't fool about with me, Tower, if you want to see those boys again.'

'I'll need some bona fides to make sure you're the right man. I don't want to hand over ten thousand in gold to the wrong man.

The man grinned, exposing broken and tobacco-stained teeth. 'You got the money, hey? Well, they's two of 'em just alike as two peas. There's another 'un talks funny. He yours too?'

'He's the son of a friend. All right, I guess you're

the one.' He started to reach into the buckboard boot, but hesitated. 'I'm going to get the gold. Don't shoot.'

'I won't shoot. Just toss it on down here.' He looked at Ben and tilted his head thoughtfully. 'But don't try nothin'. This here scattergun is serious.'

Ben lifted the heavy valise with both hands, and tossed it down to the still-grinning man, who grabbed it with one hand while the other held the shotgun on Ben. He dragged it over by the pine, where he licked his lips in anticipation, his eyes darting from Ben to the bag. At last, greed overcame his caution, so he propped his shotgun against the tree and turned the clasp on the bag, throwing it open. For a long moment, he stared at the collection of rusty nuts, bolt, and washers, with unbelieving eyes. Then he slowly turned to look at Ben who was looking back at him over the barrel of his Winchester.

'What the hell are you doin', Tower? If I don't come back with the money, them boys will be dead!'

Ben kept the steady, black cold eye of the Winchester on the kidnapper's chest, and called out loudly.

'Medicine Hawk!'

The barrel-chested Indian stepped out from the brush on the far side of the road and fixed the man with a menacing, black-eyed stare. He was naked except for a breechclout and a large knife in a sheath. He was covered in shiny bear grease, which served to accentuate his sinewy muscles and dark skin. The kidnapper glanced from Ben to Medicine Hawk and licked his lips nervously.

'Who's he? Where the hell did he come from?'

'He came well in advance and he's probably been watching you for a good half hour. He has his ways, and he sets a lot of store by those boys.' Ben pulled a set of irons from the buckboard boot and tossed them to the man.

'Put those on.'

'Hell if I will!'

Ben casually fired one round from his rifle, taking the hat off the man's head.

'I said put them on, and be quick about it!'

Ben checked the chains binding the man to the tree and nodded at Medicine Hawk who had a hot, mesquite fire going. He walked to the buckboard and pulled out two branding irons, handing them to Medicine Hawk, who placed them in the coals of his fire. He then turned to the kidnapper.

'Where are my boys? You might as well tell me now, because in due time, you'll tell me anything I want to know. In due time, you'll curse your mother if asked.'

'If I ain't back in an hour, my brother will kill them boys.' He glanced nervously from Ben to Medicine Hawk.

'Have it your way.' Ben climbed back onto the buckboard and picked up the reins, and began turning the rig around.

'Where the hell you goin'?' The kidnapper was almost frantic.

'He likes to work alone. I'll be back in the morning.' He flicked the reins and began to drive away as Medicine Hawk lifted a glowing iron from the coals of the mesquite fire with a menacing scowl.

'Wait! Wait! Stop! I'll tell you whatever you want to know, only don't leave me here alone with him! It ain't human!' The kidnapper was almost screaming in terror.

His name was Roy Stiles, older brother to Junior Styles, a ranch-hand Ben had fired the previous year for stealing a saddle. In a few minutes, and aided by an occasional dark look from Medicine Hawk, Ben knew where the boys were being held and that the Stiles brothers had acted alone.

# 14

Junior Styles was having trouble rolling himself a Mexican-style cigarette because his hands were shaking so badly. He'd committed lots of petty crimes, but this was different. His brother Roy had assured him that they could not get caught, but Roy had already spent four years in the territorial prison because he did get caught. Junior Styles did not want to go to prison.

Things had gone wrong from the start. They'd been watching the ranch with a spyglass, so when the twins were seen with fishing gear, the plot was set in motion. Junior knew where they liked to fish from his days as ranch-hand, so the Styles brothers were waiting for them. That's when they discovered the presence of a third boy with a foreign accent, and Junior was ready to drop the whole thing, but Roy wouldn't have it, so they stepped out of concealment and forced all three into the back of the stolen team and wagon at gunpoint where they were bound tightly and covered with canvas. Then Junior drove them a few miles to this place where they had already dug a shallow grave.

Learning that Roy wanted that grave dug was what alarmed Junior. Why dig a grave unless Roy planned on killing the boys either way? That, of course would be murder, and a cold-blooded, heinous murder at that. Such an outrage would certainly end in a hanging and Junior Styles also didn't want to hang, so he was contemplating his next move, and that involved abandoning his brother, not that they had ever been close. In fact, Junior never much cared for Roy anyway, because he had bullied his younger brother unmercifully when they were boys.

He checked his pocket-watch one more time. Roy was now over an hour late, so he made up his mind and untied his riding horse from the back of the wagon. He started to rein him around and then hesitated. He stepped back down, and pulled the canvas off the boys who stared back at him. Then he fished around in his saddle bags and pulled out his old spare pocket-knife.

'I'm done with this damn thing, boys, so I'm riding off. I'm leaving this here knife so's you can cut your bindings in due time.'

He spat over his shoulder.

'Truth be told, I didn't want nothing to do with this sorry adventure from the jump, but I reckon I'm a cowardly sort and scared of my brother, so I did what he told me.'

He took off his hat and wiped the sweatband.

'Tell your pa what I said about wanting no part of this. He was real good to me, and then I up and stole a saddle from him. Damn me for being a thief. I regret that one too.' With that, Junior Styles mounted up and headed for the distant blue mountains.

Half an hour later, the boys were free and rubbing their wrists. The team was still hitched to the wagon, so they decided to just drive it back to the ranch. Joseph climbed into the seat and was picking up the reins when he spotted a rifle. He checked it and it was loaded. He was about to tell the others when he heard approaching hoofs.

'Horse coming! Run and hide behind that brush pile over there!'

Joseph grabbed the rifle and dove behind the brush with the others. Then he laid the rifle across the brush and eared back the hammer.

'What are you going to do?'

'Look down and under this brush pile. What do you see?'

Jeremiah looked and his face paled. He glanced at his brother.

'That looks like a sure enough grave.'

Joseph nodded. 'I'm going to do what Pa taught us. Junior wasn't a real bad man I reckon, but that brother of his is as wicked as they get. I think he means to kill us, so I'm about to defend us, but if he gets me first, it's up to you, Jerry.'

Jeremiah nodded.

The sound of hoofs grew louder, and Joseph suddenly realized that there were at least two horses, maybe more. His shoulders tightened, and he wiped the sweat from his brow. Then the riders appeared and he relaxed.

'Pa! Mister Farnsworth! Uncle Bear! We're over here!'

# 15

'Tell me again what happened, Ben. Leave nothing out.'

In the west, lightning flashed silently from an approaching thunderstorm. The sun was below the horizon, but its rays lit up the dark bottom of the storm in brilliant scarlets that contrasted beautifully with inky blackness. Mattie sipped a glass of wine that had been produced on the ranch by a French family who had established a vineyard. It was surprisingly good, so she invested some of her own money in the growing business. She and Ben were seated on the south porch.

'As I said, Reggie was waiting for me just down the road and out of sight from where Medicine Hawk and I confronted Roy Styles. After Styles told me what I wanted to know, I was on my way to confront Junior Styles, so it was well that Bear took it upon himself to trail us. Three armed men are better than one.'

Ben lit a fresh cigar, and took a sip of his whiskey and water. The wind was beginning to freshen from the approaching storm and the coolness felt good. Lightning was starting to dance on the far end of the valley floor, and faint thunder now came their way.

'As it happened of course, Junior had a change of mind and left. But before he did, he gave the boys a knife so they could free themselves.' Ben looked at Mattie, whose jaw was set and hard. 'That has to count for something, Mattie.'

'Maybe.' She rose and walked to the porch railing. 'You said there was a fresh grave dug and ready?' She turned and regarded her husband quietly. He nodded but said nothing.

'They were going to kill our sons, and poor Jack too, Ben Tower. I won't rest until both of those bastards are hanging from a gallows.' It was the first time he had ever heard Mattie use profanity.

'Planning to kill and actually killing are two different things, Mattie. No court will hang them because no one died.' Ben rose and stood by Mattie, placing his big arm around her slim shoulders. The storm was building steadily, and the thunder was now almost constant. The mysterious, clean smell of new rain on parched earth, filled the air.

'I know the law won't permit it, Ben, and I would not want anyone to break the law, but as a woman and a mother, I will never be at ease until those two men are dead and rotting in their graves.'

Ben nodded. 'If they had harmed any of those

147

boys, Reggie and I would have done for them.'

'If the one called Roy had refused to talk, what would you have done?'

'I would have kept my promise, Mattie. Medicine Hawk is an Indian, and they like to see how brave a man is before he begs them to stop, and they all do beg sooner or later. Roy Styles knew he was whipped, so the way he saw it, there was no sense in being stubborn.'

The first few drops of rain sounded on the tin porch roof, but Ben and Mattie were reluctant to leave so they retreated to their chairs and side table. Ben took another sip of his drink. He allowed himself one of an evening.

'Clay Johnson and Bear took Roy Styles in irons to Harvey Davis, since he's the only real law around here. I expect he'll confess and ask the court for mercy, since it's obvious that he's guilty. He's already been in prison once, so he knows it's futile to pretend he's an innocent man. Junior will probably get caught too, but I still think he just did what his big brother told him to do. In fact, it took courage to abandon the whole thing and defy Roy.'

Mattie sighed. 'Just about the time I think you're hard as nails, you show me the soft side I saw when you buried my family. I'll trust your judgment as always, Ben.'

The rain was now coming down in earnest, and the parched earth was getting a welcome drink. Always the rancher, Ben Tower was already thinking he might get one more crop of hay in before winter thanks to this rain, as he and Mattie went inside.

'Well now, what on Earth. . . ?'

Ben looked up from his breakfast and saw Mattie gazing out the kitchen window. Ben stepped over to the window and peered out at the wagon pulling into the barnyard. It was Clay and Bear.

'Hell, this is not good. It's a two-day drive to the capital, and it has barely been a day since they left. And where's Roy Styles?'

Breakfast forgotten, Ben grabbed his hat and headed for the door. Mattie moved the heavy skillet off the hot stove and turned down the damper. She hung her apron on its hook and smoothed her dress before following her husband.

In the heat of the new day, mist was rising from the mud of the barnyard as Ben strode rapidly to the wagon where Bear and Clay waited.

'It was the damnedest thing I ever saw, Boss.' Bear shook his head.

'Where's Styles?'

Clay jerked his head at the wagon-bed so Ben walked to the rear and stared at the two bodies as Clay and Bear climbed down from the seat. Clay looked at Bear who began to speak.

'We was crossin' a dry streambed about twenty-five mile from here when we saw the smoke of a camp-fire and smelled coffee. It was time to spell the horses anyway, so we pulled off and was just gettin' down when Junior Styles stepped out of the brush with a shotgun and pulled down on us.'

Mattie, who had just joined the group, gasped and turned to leave. 'I need to see to the boys!' Ben took her arm gently and shook his head. 'There's no need to worry, Mattie. Let's hear what Clay and Bear have to say.'

'Turned out that Junior saw us comin' and realized we had his brother, so he braced us with that there scatter-gun and disarmed us. Roy wanted Junior to remove the irons, but Junior paid him no never-mind at all. That made Roy just awful mad, but like I said, Junior acted like he couldn't hear him. He walked Roy over to a big oak and tied his irons off to the trunk with a piece of rope. Then he come back to the wagon and made us drive on down the road a piece with him sittin' in the bed behind us. I figured he was goin' to do for both of us, but after a spell, he made us get down and muttered somethin' about waitin' an hour before followin' him. Then he just turned that rig around and went back.'

Bear looked to Clay for confirmation. Clay nodded and motioned for Bear to continue.

'Well, we done what he wanted and headed back after an hour or so. It took us another half hour or so to return to the camp and then we saw seen the damnedest thing ever ... beggin' your pardon, Mattie, for my rough words.'

Mattie shrugged. 'I've heard far worse almost every day. After all, this is a ranch. Go on with your story.'

Bear nodded. 'Well, there was Roy Styles, hangin' by his neck from a limb of that there big oak, dead as dead can be, and sittin' up there on that same limb was his brother, Junior, with a rope around his own neck and the other end tied off to the same limb. He said to tell you folks that he was plumb sorry about what he and his brother had done after you both was so good to him and then he just slid off and hung himself.'

Clay nodded. 'Me and Bear couldn't do a thing to stop him and he was dead as soon as he hit the end of that rope. I know that they were both bad men, but it was an awful thing to see, just the same. They won't be botherin' you or them boys ever again, Mattie. Both of them are back there in the wagon bed.'

Ben regarded his wife for a moment. 'Well, looks like you got your wish, Mattie. Both of those bastards got hung after all.'

Mattie walked to the back of the wagon and after a few moments, returned to her husband.

'I don't want them buried on the Rafter T, Ben. I don't mean to be contrary or petty, but I want them taken far away. They kidnapped my sons, and planned on killing them. Please do this one thing for me. It's important.'

Ben nodded his agreement.

'Have Johnny and Drew take them up to Marshal Harvey Davis, Bear. I'll write Harvey a letter explaining what happened. He can have them buried in the prison cemetery.'

He turned to leave and then paused.

'You'd best have Joe make up a box to put them in and seal it up good with tar and pitch, inside and out. It's still summer and hot.'

# 16

Mattie sat in her rocker and watched the branding from the porch as she did her knitting. Her habit of wearing a bonnet, veil, and gloves all these years had spared her the raw, sunburned skin and leathery wrinkles of many other women her age and her hair was still black as coal except for a few odd strands of pure white scattered about. Socialites who saw her and Ben attending some event, thought Ben had married a woman half his age and secretly it pleased her immensely.

The twins, Joseph and Jeremiah, now twenty-one and men grown, paired off as ropers while their younger brothers, Walt, nineteen and Henry, seventeen, helped the other hands work the irons and fires. Julie, the youngest at sixteen and the lone girl, sat with her father on the rails and made the tally.

The house was low and rambling, the result of rooms added on through the years as the children came. The walls were solid timbers, cool of a summer and warm when the stoves glowed a cherry-red in the winter. Two large barns housed the horses and milking cattle. The barns' haymows, normally full to the rafters, were nearly empty after a harsh winter, but the tall, spring grasses promised a bumper crop. The spring calving had been better than expected and the herd was due to be thinned soon by a large shipment to satisfy a contract with a meat packer in Kansas City.

The original cabin was now occupied by Bear, or Uncle Bear as the children had come to call him. He protested that he was nobody's uncle, but Mattie knew he was pleased to be thought of as family. Although he was now in his seventies, Mattie could see him hazing calves toward the corrals for branding.

Ben, a tireless worker, had become an accomplished and shrewd businessman, and a good provider for his family. Together with Mattie, he had fought off land jumpers, high graders, and occasional cattle thieves. There had been talk of Ben running for office, but he turned them down. His life was his family and the empire known as the Rafter T.

The small village of Cook's Crossing was now a ghost town; just a collection of abandoned buildings and Ben had bought back most of the properties. The railroad had long since gone through to the north and most immigrants now came in by rail, leaving Cook's Crossing without a good reason for being.

Ben also bought out the sawmill and moved it to the ranch where he built a dam on the western slope to provide water power for the giant blade. Later, he brought in a far more efficient steam engine. He was now under contract to the railroad for additional ties and bridge timbers for all the new spurs being put in. He had also secured deeds for vast areas of timber far up the northern slopes by convincing the Governor that he could produce the needed lumber. His word was well-respected and the Governor ordered the State land deeded over to Ben for mere dollars to the acre.

To the south was the small, neat town that housed the timber jacks, miners, shop owners, ranch-hands and all their families. There was a general store, a blacksmith shop, a post office, two saloons, a school and a church. The pastor was the same Preacher Hanson who had married Ben and Mattie. His wife was the school teacher and had taught all the Tower children.

Once a month, Ben had his teamsters take wagons north to Berryville to deliver timber and pick up supplies and mail. The railroad was building a spur all the way to the sawmill as part of the timber contract, and there was talk of building a town where the Rafter T spur connected with the main line along with two other spurs. Ben and Mattie had talked it over and decided that if the town came to be, they would invest in a business or two to help get it on its feet.

Mattie rose and went in to check on the noon meal. One of Ben's cowhands had foolishly admitted that he was a fair cook and he had been stuck in the kitchen ever since, replacing a forever-grateful Clay Johnson. Big Farley Chatsworth had been a chef in Saint Louis before he had ventured west as a cowhand and once his secret was out, the other hands wouldn't allow him to sit on a horse unless he was going for kitchen supplies. He was considered the most valuable hand on the ranch, bar none, and anything he wanted for the kitchen was immediately sent for, no matter how far off or expensive it might be. The Rafter T ranch-house dining room was considered the best place to eat, east of San Francisco and west of Kansas City.

Chatsworth looked up as Mattie entered the kitchen. 'It's ready, ma'am, if you want to call them in.' He nodded his head at the clock which stood at 12:00, high noon.

Mattie walked to the back porch and tugged on the dinner-bell rope. Before the echoes died away, the ranch-hands were already elbow deep in the row of wash basins set up by the well pump. Mattie smiled at the good-natured ribbing and chatter from the hands, from Ben, the boys, and her daughter, Julie. One by one they dried off on the racked towels and filed in to sit at the big table.

Julie always gave as good as she got. Like her mother, she was a lady at all times, but she could also hold her own with her rowdy brothers. She had spurned the sidesaddle as a child and called it silly, dangerous and unsuitable for a ranch girl. Mattie agreed reluctantly but soon followed suit and found the regular saddle far more practical and never used the sidesaddle again. It started a trend that quickly spread to the other wives and daughters on the ranch. After all, Mattie had ridden astride when Ben had brought her to the Rafter T so long ago, so why not now?

Mattie adored her daughter and it took all her will power not to spoil her or dote on her, although Ben spoiled her enough for both of them. Even then, Julie asked for little and gave the ranch her all. She was as much a top hand as any of her brothers and they all knew it and respected her for it.

Because of that, the brothers were all stunned when she came out of her bedroom early one evening, dressed for a dance at the school. They suddenly realized that their little sister was also a beautiful, young lady. Consequently, when her unsuspecting beau came to pick her up in a carriage, the brothers had a private moment with him outside. He drove away with the firm understanding that it would be very unhealthy to make her unhappy in any way or forget, even for a moment, that she was a lady.

Mattie entered the dining room and quietly took her place at the end of the table opposite Ben as the hungry hands and her children waited patiently and respectfully. After she was seated, Ben bowed his head and said grace. The hands added their solemn amens, and then the table exploded in a noisy frenzy of laughter and talk as the big platters made their way around the table.

Ben joined Mattie on the porch after dinner and lit his pipe. His gray hair was thinning, and he had taken to cutting it short. She had noticed that while he still did a day's work, his workday was shorter than it used to be and the work not so strenuous as it once had been.

For a long time, they watched the branding in silence. Finally, Ben spoke without turning his head.

'We've come a long way from that day on the prairie, Mattie, and we did what we set out to do. I said back then I had big plans, but even as a young man, I never imagined it would be this big. You made all the difference and that's a fact.'

Mattie folded her knitting and placed it on the table beside her. After a moment, she rose and moved behind her husband, placing her hands on his broad shoulders. 'You've been a good man, a good husband, and a good father to my children, Ben. I thank the Good Lord that it was you who found me that day.'

Ben chuckled and patted her small hand. 'What could I do? You had the big rifle pointed at me.'

Mattie smiled and kissed his graying head. 'Yes, but it wasn't loaded, dear.'